the Touch

EMILY FOREMAN

CLAY BRIDGES
PRESS

Dedicated to my Creator,
my Sustainer,
my Lord,
my Hero,
my King,
my Heart,
my Love

Contents

The Touch

I didn't die the way most people say you do. Or perhaps I should say, I didn't enter into and find myself in death in the same way many people describe it happening. I didn't ascend from my body and look down at my own lifeless form or float through a dark tunnel, following a bright light at the end of it. However, there was a light, and it was quite bright. It was the most startlingly brilliant light that I had ever seen. But unlike all other dazzling lights, it was not blinding. I could look straight into its source and rather than being forced to look away, my eyes seemed to be opened to a new capacity, enabling me to see things that I had not seen before and to absorb the place in which I found myself with more clarity.

The place itself was soft—not soft to the touch or like the billowing, bouncing clouds that naked babies were said to leap upon in Heaven, but soft to my soul and my spirit. Though I found my physical body gone, my senses were still very much there. And my form, though different some-how, was very much with me. I felt softness in my mouth, between my molars and on my tongue. Softness encircled my eyes and touched my retina at the same time as my ears heard softness, and my lips were brushed with it. The skin on my shoulders and the bottoms of my feet and forehead were loosened and relaxed, as if a belt had been unnotched, surrendering to the space that demanded a full breath to be inhaled.

The softness was the realest thing present, yet through this veneer of lush delicacy, my newly enhanced sight recognized the outline of a meadow. I sensed heather and long blades of golden grass synchronized in waves that seemed to be pro-pelled by the dazzling rays themselves rather than by a breeze or wind. The movement in the air wrapped itself around each strand of hair and every budding flower, and it carried the softness to them. The meadow was in flux with the emergence of new growth and life recurring several times within one blink of the eye. But just as quickly as one shoot would spring forth, another would curl its head and return to the ground.

The light seemed to move into every part of what was once called my body, and I began to feel each cell within my being expand, like a raisin that has been dropped into a cup of warm water. Just as a mother would wake her sleeping child, the light kissed each molecule, fiber, and atom and bade my body arise from its slumber. The parts of my being that once felt, saw, heard, tasted, and smelled remained with me, but their sensations became, not just magnified, but entirely new. Their reach and capacity were enhanced with a depth that, unfortunately, could never be described using the non-expansive vocabulary or comprehension from human experience.

*   *   *

I feel myself being enveloped into this softness that welcomes me out of what now feels like a cramped shell. My body responds, unfolding and filling up like a bouncy house coming out of storage. I feel as though, finally, I am experiencing what it means to come alive . The light softens and massages the muscles of my form, and they too billow in strength and energy that had never before existed in their capsuled state. I am full.

As my eyes adjust to the new depth of their full scope of vision, I begin to see the light take form. Just as I step out of my former capacities, this radiance is transformed (or perhaps, it is finally perceived for what it always was), and I become aware that the light is far more than what it first appeared to be. The brilliant, nonblinding light is suddenly glistening with both the reflection of a lake's surface and the exquisite smoothness of a bolt of silk. And like a bolt of silk, were it rolled down a flight of stairs, the light falls gracefully from a height that my eyes cannot yet see. Its smooth edges meet their end with the beginning of my bare feet, and the light, without arms or words, pulls me onto its silken train, drawing me in while embracing me with its glorious warmth and abundance.

"Come," the light says, "and see."

I do not respond to the invitation. I am uncertain whether it is for a loss of words or the inability to speak that my voice remains silent, but the light that had entered into and taken up residency within my form moves the reigns from where they once were held tightly within my mind's grasp and places them in the shared control of each cell of my being. In unison, they respond for me with an exuberant acceptance of the light's summoning, and I step onto the perfect path of soft, flowing brilliance.

I move steadily, held by my form that at long last is given the ability to speak and move in accordance with its true desire. I am no longer the master of my frame, which rejoices in freedom and ease. I, the being, remain reserved, but each part of me, independent of my foremost knowing, yearns to reach the end of the lightened path.

"This is where we came from, and this is where we belong," they seem to sing. The song is alien to me, and yet I somehow know the words.

The silken path never seems to end; still, I find myself at the base of a towering marble wall that possesses a surface smoother than the place upon which I tread, reflecting a vibrancy equal to that of the light. I can at last, with fully opened eyes, see the top of this astonishing stronghold upon which a single throne sits. The throne is empty, waiting quietly at an unattainable height. For reasons I don't understand, I feel an immense grief wash over each hopeful cell in my body, and I begin to weep, kneeling at the base of the beautiful, perfect fortress that keeps me from the Glory that my body somehow knows it was made for. As I kneel upon the lightened path at the base of the wall in devastation, I hear small feet running toward me. Startled, I look up just in time to see the blur of a small figure, hair streaming and arms extended, fly past me. The child, for indeed it was a young girl, veers away from the wall and runs straight toward an abyss that I had not seen just moments ago. She disappears suddenly, almost as if the ground beneath her had given way.

I venture forward to find that, indeed, the path ends abruptly, and a chasm, too great for description, stretches between the rest of the Glorious towering wall and me. I look to the horizon and see, just past the depths of the abyss, a small, humble threshold—a way into whatever lies behind this solid structure of Glory. The faintest ember of hope dances inside me until I look again into the chasm that stretches before me at the base of this abrupt cliff. A looming darkness ebbs in and around its perimeter, like flames feeling for an energy source to ignite.

At the center, a figure stands. He emits the enveloping softness and light that, not only cloaks His form, but is being woven and expanded by His presence. Light and softness cascade from His head and crash repeatedly into the pool of darkness below, pushing it back, like a cleansing wave.

His countenance is fiercely glorious and threatening. I watch, with new vision, as the small child, who had disappeared over the edge of the cliff deep within the depths of the valley, approaches. As she turns toward the countenance of the Brilliant One, her face is kissed on the cheeks, forehead, and nose by the light, just as a ray would land upon her skin at the seaside. As the light shines upon her, the little girl's face becomes illuminated and threatening, reflecting the ferocity that was first realized within the face of the Brilliant one from which the light was first born. As the little one approaches, the darkness advances toward her, reaching aggressively with tendrils that are eager to pull her into its vacuum. Just as the light on her face expands to illuminate her whole being, the grasping claws of the black body reaches out and closes around her leg. Immediately, the darkness withdraws, letting out a shriek as if it itself had been burned.

I see the arms of the Brilliant Being extend toward the small figure, and she runs, without hesitation, into His arms. As they embrace, many wounds the size of paper cuts become apparent to me. They cover her body from the top of her cheekbone to the soles of her feet. Though each gash is small and barely noticeable, they are, nevertheless, numerous. I wait, anticipating the goodness and softness of the brilliant light to make the Ebenezers of her hurt vanish as if they had never been there. The young girl's hands and those of the Brilliant Being are clasped; her head, resting heavy on the chest of the One who holds her. As she softens herself into His arms, the tiny cuts grow in size and depth. Blood begins to pour from her wounds as though a hunting knife had slashed through the center of each one. She collapses in pain, intuitively pushing away from the arms that embrace her. The full realization of the depth of her pain had come from her union with the Brilliant Being, and it seemed far too much to bear. She begins to wail, unable to absorb the agony of each seemingly minuscule hurt, now being brought to its full realization. Her body, once a myriad of tiny, seemingly insignificant scars, pours forth a fountain of blood, evidence of a far more profound pain and harm than initially perceived. The Brilliant Being stretches His arms toward her with confidence, gripping both her triceps firmly as she presses away from the apparent source of her pain. Determined, He hugs her into His chest.

They weep in the profound revelation of what lay beneath her lacerations, tears streaming from both of their radiant eyes. As the tears fall, one by one, the wounds multiply, covering, the soft, luminous skin of the Being. They sit together, embraced in a mutual comprehension of the intensity of her wounds, until slowly, reverently, the bleeding from each slash ceases. Instead of the red syrupy drops, a light of proportionate glory, which flows like water but travels like clouds, begins to emit from her many wounds, and she is at once enraptured in the same softness and beauty that pours unceasingly from the Brilliant One. Her wounds become the source of pure light, and she melts once again into the embrace of the Being whose hold never broke; in strength they rise to their feet. For a moment, her small head lays heavy on His chest, and then, as if prompted by the change in direction of a phantom wind, she vanishes into light.

I watch, frightened and in awe. The Being turns His eyes upon me, and I feel the silken path of light startle as

though His gaze had sent a quake through its core. I try to
look away, but my eyes won't let me. They see what they've
desired, and they will not turn from it. The Being extends
His hand toward me, and beckons me to step farther into the
valley, closer to Him. The darkness swirls, also beckoning, if
not daring, that I tread into its depths. I make a step against
my will, and I feel a strong grip around my ankle. I cry out
in shock and immediately feel another claw-like grasp clutch
my arm, seemingly from the formless darkness. I fear I am
about to be enveloped by the void, and in desperation, I look
up, instinctively seeking aid from the source of light that
stood ahead of me on the path that I sought to walk down.
As my eyes land on Him, I feel the grip of the tendrils loosen
and then disappear altogether. And in the next moment,
I am propelled through the depths of the chasm. I find
myself standing before the Being, His terrifying gaze, ever
fixed and overwhelming.

He extends His hands and, in a voice that booms like
colliding heat waves, He asks, "Will you let Me touch you?"

I stand, open-mouthed and unable to speak. His eyes
move to my chest, and I follow His gaze. There, a gaping wound as large as my fist gushes forth blood while the
heart in my chest cavity, exposed and vulnerable, pumps
irregularly and weakly. I look up in shock, baffled by my
complete unawareness of this fatal wound. I reach toward
my mutilated heart, bewildered by the state of it, but stop
short when I see that my hands are scarlet red, dripping
with a thick, viscous substance that I can only assume is

blood. I shriek, disoriented entirely by what is happening. It is the shriek of one who has just wildly plunged a knife into the chest of another human and the shriek of the one whose chest has been violently pierced with the steel blade. I am both the perpetrator and victim in this instance, and I collapse to the ground, holding my wound with my blood-soaked hands.

"What do you want from me?" I cry, as I begin to sob from the torment of exposure and the discomfort of guilt.

"You."

A distrusting snarl curls down from the top of the chasm, and I lift my gaze to see the suspicious eyes of a frail woman darting from one end of the valley to the other but not once landing on the Brilliant Being. Although her body is poised to flee, her figure is hardly whole. One arm seems to be dislocated and would sag toward the ground if it weren't for the other arm that cradled it. Her foot and leg of the opposite side are crushed so that when she walks, she must drag her foot through the dust. The flesh on her face is burned badly, and tufts of her hair are missing on the sides and top of her head. She snarls again, puss spewing from the wounds surrounding her mouth.

"Once it touches you, you are never the same. It takes everything and leaves nothing. You are a fool if you let it near!" she warns.

The gaze of the Brilliant Being does not move away from my face, and yet He looks toward the woman who stands above us at the top of the steep embankment. The air is still;

no sounds break the silence that settled after the words she spoke, but as if in response to an unspoken question, the woman shrieks, "Never!"

She turns, hobbling away as quickly as her crippled leg will allow.

The Brilliant Being is at once at the woman's side, pursuing her but not hindering her departure. He persists, nearly shoulder to shoulder with her, until she can no longer run. She bends her body into an exhausted slump that resembles the form one might take while trying to catch their breath. Again, I hear nothing, but the woman startles suddenly and clutches her wounded arm to her chest as if it were a crying infant.

"I will not yield! There is no part of me that You can have!"

She spits, somehow not surprised but nevertheless indignant to see the Brilliant Being standing right by her side. She then releases her dislocated arm, winds up her other, and strikes the Brilliant Being across the face.

"You are false!" she cries, "and a liar!" I remain frozen, watching in shock as He stands silent before her. "I know who You are," she says, pointing a bony claw at His face. "And I know what it is You want. You want it all—my freedom, my name, my truth! But You shall not touch it. It is mine and mine alone."

His eyes fill with tears, and I see reflected in them a hunger so deep that I thought it would devour her. The Brilliant Being desired this woman to give herself to Him more than I could comprehend, and yet He would not advance past the line in the sand she had drawn. I see unparalleled pain mark His face; it is the excruciating ache of love lost and truth forgotten, but the woman seems blind to the apparent desire He has for her. She spits at His feet and turns away, walking toward the darkness; its tendrils do not reach for her. On the contrary, the surface is still and uninviting, like a bottomless black lake. Her presence invokes no response from the void as she approaches, and in a half whisper, half hiss, she says, "At last. I'm safe."

In the same moment that these words depart from her lips, she collapses in on her own being, like an empty cardboard box being broken down to reveal its hollow center. The Being advances toward the edge of the darkness into which she disappeared, and He kneels at its border. His presence pushes the darkness back, like the luminous glow of a candle spreads an orb of light in the dark room in which it shines. And there, where I had seen the woman submerge herself beneath the surface of the void, lay a *name*—like a seashell in the sand left behind by the waves at the ocean. I cannot describe what a *name* looks like, but I knew what it was when I saw it. The Brilliant Being takes up her Lost Name, and holding it gently in His palms, presses it to His chest, bowing His head with a sorrow so heavy that I wondered whether His eyes would ever be lifted again.

I stand bewildered by such a profound display of grief coming from this Being—this mighty and terrifying entity. The loss of the woman was great, and His mourning of her reflected this. I knew that her name, held reverently in

His palms, would never be forgotten. Indeed, this moment stood still with no calculable second, minute, or hour with which to measure it. This instance was not frozen, for it continued onward in a trajectory I did not understand, for there was no time at all with which this moment would be contained. The Being kneels there, cradling the Lost Name with untold reverence and longing, unyielding to the darkness.

I am jolted out of my marveling when I suddenly hear the voice of the Being, still by my side, ask me again, "Will you let me touch you?"

He stands with His hand extended toward my mutilated chest, His fingertips hovering just over the exposed wound. I am terrified to answer. I know somehow that rejecting His request would not incite any harm from the hand now extended toward me, and yet I fear, with everything in me, what it would mean to accept His invitation. Still, I feel the emptiness within my core whirl dangerously, as though a tiny tornado had been stirred up to remind me of the barren space within my being. I could choose to put the full weight of all I'd done and all that had been done to me on my own shoulders. But just as the woman who had entrusted her wounds and wounding to her own frame had collapsed, I too would cave beneath my own weight if I made that same choice. I could not advance toward Him or even meet His gaze to invite Him in. Yet I felt the tiniest pieces of my being uniting in solidarity to compose this intercession, "Have Your way."

And no sooner were those words on my tongue, than His hand was upon my wound.

I cannot explain what happened next in any form other than that of a story. But you must understand that what will soon be revealed to you as a series of vignettes was not revealed to me in the same way. In the instant that The Touch met my wound, it called forth my entire history as though it had always been a part of my memory and mind. I was not walked through the following instances as if they were a new experience to be gained. Rather, just as my eyes, muscles, and very essence had been expanded and augmented, so did my memories evolve and unfold in such a way that I fully felt, saw, and recalled these stories in a split-second as if they were my own.

Although I had never fully known or been physically present for the stories I'm about to share, I nevertheless knew them to be a part of me. To help you understand how each of these moments is related to one another, I will share them in reverse chronological order, beginning with the following formative experiences that shaped both my life and my person while I was still alive on earth.

Giftless

It was Sunday. The most dreaded day of the week. The tumult and stress that traditionally was a part of my family's morning routine seemed to be heightened on Sundays, making the proportionate increase in fake smiles and overwhipped confections of verbal greetings and salutations all the more unbearable. My sister, brother, and I would emerge from a house filled with criticism over acceptable church attire and drama from delay in departure; nevertheless, we were expected to slide seamlessly into the church pew with plastic smiles and the joy of the Lord in our hearts. We felt the incongruence deeply and struggled to combat the honest voices in our spirits and minds that yelled, "This is not the way it is supposed to be!"

Our father, being an elder of the church, felt extra pressure to appear a certain way, and that certain way demanded that we dress, speak, and act "nicely." We were his homework papers that would be scrutinized by his fellow Christians, and my father was determined to never receive a bad grade. He himself was a very "nice" man who would receive a huge amount of flattery when people spoke about him to my brother, sister, and me.

"Your father is such a kind soul," they would say. "I've never met a man so sincere a Christian as your father."

And to pay credit to their astuteness, our father did take his title as Christian very seriously. My mother played her role well. It's no wonder she was given the part of charitable, devout, God-fearing wife some fifteen years ago when our father asked her to marry him. She fit the part and never stepped out of character. Her smile seemed sincere, and her warm words seemed honest when we would watch her press the hand of an older, frail woman between her palms and attentively listen to the earnest prayer requests for her "spiritually lost" grandson. But we knew better. We had watched her, just minutes before this interaction, as we sat in our car in the church parking lot, scream at us to, "Just listen to your God damn father and quit bickering!"

As soon as we emerged from our car and shut the doors, the scene would be set, and we would each take our positions. It often felt fitting for someone to yell, "Action!" as if we were on a movie set, so inauthentic were our roles.

This particular Sunday was one that I had looked forward to, however. It was the church's annual children's talent show. Anyone between the ages of four and fourteen was allowed to participate, and the limitations of what one was allowed to share as their talent were endless. Or at least, they were said to be. Of course, there were the unspoken rules that prohibited sharing anything that was lurid or provocative, distasteful, trashy or "secular" as defined by our church collectively. My father had pulled me aside after the morning church service when the upcoming Talent Show was announced and told me that I was free to be a part of the event, provided that what I chose to share was a "real talent."

"This is to be a tasteful event," said he, "and I do not want you to do anything silly."

Though his words were vague, I knew exactly what he meant. Do something to make him proud or do nothing at all. There was to be no display of mediocrity. Embarrassing him with something that was below the church's standards was a possibility that I don't think even entered his mind as a viable danger. He had taught us better. Or so he thought.

Up until that morning, I had decided that I would not be performing at the talent show. This was not my part in the family. My younger, smarter, and frankly, more talented sister was the main attraction in our family's line up of prodigy. She could sing like Charlotte Church, tap dance like she was on a mission to put the ant species on the verge of extinction, and she regularly made the old men who sat on the front row of the church every Sunday morning cry when she would play the violin at the opening of the service. My sister had in fact herself been brought to tears the night before over the mere fact that she could only choose *one* of her many talents to share. I on the other hand knew how to swing a bat and climb a tree. But there were none growing on the front stage of the sanctuary, and we were surrounded by stained glass windows.

So, there I sat, hands folded neatly in my lap, content to simply enjoy the alternative and far more entertaining spectacles than what we normally experienced on Sunday mornings. A young girl in a sky-blue dress with periwinkle flowers had just taken a modest curtsy after opening the show by demonstrating sign language to every verse of the hymn, "That Old Rugged Cross." I clapped, somewhat disengaged, until I noticed Mrs. Clark, the pastor's wife, lift a small mesh necklace, wrapped around several small trinkets that were sectioned and tied off with mini bows, from a basket. She placed it over the head of the girl who had just given her performance and patted her shoulder in affirmation before resuming her clapping. My back straightened when I realized that the small trinkets inside the mesh necklace were pieces of candy. If it were to be put mildly, you could say I had a strong affinity for it, but in truth, the stuff was entirely irresistible to me. I would do almost anything for sugar, including suffer my father's disapproval or even wrath.

So, when Mrs. Clark turned to the congregation and asked, "Now, who else would be so generous as to bless us with their God-given gifts?"

I, without even realizing it, stuck my arm straight in the air.

"Oh, yes! Thank you! Please come on up!" Mrs. Clark said, smiling warmly at me.

I felt entirely out of control of my body at this point, which was driven purely by a deep desire for the mesh necklace stuffed with candy. I had no clue what I was going to do once I arrived on stage, and with each step, I felt a growing anxiety about what was about to happen. Still, the desire for the satiation of my sweet tooth prevailed, and I found myself at center stage, waiting for a wave of inspiration to overtake me.

Then, the unthinkable happened. I opened my mouth and out came the words, "Knock, knock."

The congregation rallied, seemingly excited to be a part of the production, and in unison responded, "Who's there?"

A large smile spread over my face. "Cargo."

Everyone was on edge. "Cargo, who?"

I had them where I wanted them. "Cargo beep, beep, vroom!"

Laughter erupted in the sanctuary, and I was convinced at this point that participating in the talent show was actually a very good decision. Their positive response emboldened me, and I pressed on.

"Knock, knock!"

Everyone was eager for another and with gusto asked, "Who's there?"

I could barely get the word out, as I was about to burst into hysterical laughter. "Goliath!"

People could hardly stand the anticipation. "Goliath who?!"

I'm bursting with pride over my captivation of the audience. "Go lieth thee down, thou lookest tired!"

This one had people doubled over. A real zinger and a Bible joke to boot! Tears from laughter streamed down the cheeks of the older men, and even the young kids who didn't get it were giggling over the ridiculous display of the adults. I dared a glance at my father and saw that even he was smiling, seemingly proud of the show I was putting on.

I felt one more joke percolating, and just as the raucous hoots and hollers started to die down, I let out another, "Knock, knock!"

They answered, "Who's there?"

"Brittney Spears!"

The enthusiasm was extinguished like a candle on a birthday cake. A few stray responses of "Who's there?" made it out of the congregation, giving me just enough fumes in my tank to limp along to the finish line.

"Knock, knock," I said again. Everyone seemed to be confused.

"Who's there?" was offered by even fewer in the audience.

I delivered my punch line with as much gusto as the others and shouted, "Oops! I did it again!"

You could have heard a pin drop on the floor. The room was silent. I stood with my arms open, hoping for some sort of response from the room full of people who were in the palm of my hand just moments before. Most of the faces looking back at me were so full of disdain that I couldn't help but feel that they'd like to squish me like a bug. I had crossed the line into secular man's land and, apparently, there was no going back.

Mrs. Clark stood up from her chair in the corner of the stage and began to clap her hands weakly, doing her best to pick up the pieces of the talent show.

Remembering my motivation for coming on stage in the first place, I scurried toward her, a hot wave of shame spreading from my forehead to the rest of my body. I stole a glance at my dad from the corner of my eye as Mrs. Clark placed the mesh candy necklace over my head. His face was stony; his eyes flashing with a rage that I knew very well. I'd trespassed onto his good reputation, and I would pay dearly for it. Mrs. Clark patted my shoulder reassuringly as I climbed down from the stage, feeling like an immense failure and embarrassment.

My family held it together for the rest of the morning; my mother's pleasant demeanor was plastered on her face like a clown's red and white smile. My father laughed congenially and nodded his head in seeming agreement with every individual who approached him after the show to congratulate him on the natural-born comedian in his family. Everyone acted as though the awkward incident involving the mention of a secular icon in the middle of a children's show had never happened. Even my sister, who I could tell was exceedingly miffed at me for making an appearance on stage before she did, kept her cool and stayed in character. It wasn't until after we had climbed into our golden Dodge Caravan and the last door had been shut that the volcanic eruption finally came.

"I am incredibly disappointed in you!" my father said,

pushing the key into the ignition and turning it with agitation. "You intentionally defied my very clear instructions. Was I not clear?"

My dad's eyes were popping out of his red head as he swiveled around, his right arm pressing against the back of the passenger seat as he tried to back out of our parking space. My dad's voice rose in volume, and his animation grew in intensity the farther we drove from the church.

"I am your authority, and you chose to directly disobey me. I would not be loving you if I let this go unpunished!"

I sat with my head lowered, fixing my gaze on a sheet of half-used sticker words that said things like, "Hallelujah!" "Jesus is king!" "Glory to God!" "Jesus loves you!" and "Praise!" on the floor of the car.

"You chose to trust your own foolishness and follow the sinful desires of your heart for attention over the loving voice of your father. It was a stupid decision you made. You will know after tonight, that walking down destructive paths like the one you chose this morning will never end in prosperity!"

My dad began to settle down, feeling the pressure that had been building from the moment of my performance finally get released as he spewed his words of judgment on me with venom.

After my father had thoroughly spent his rage, my mother, who had sat quietly looking out the passenger window up until that point, murmured, "If you would like to become talented, you're going to need to put in a lot more effort than you have."

"Yeah," piped up my younger sister, who was still indignant at my presumptuousness in taking up space on stage. A place that had historically been her stomping ground. "Do you have any idea how much time I spend practicing all my talents?"

I slumped my shoulders a little lower, trying to somehow vanish into the crack where the seat and back support of the Dodge's captain's chair came together. I knew there would be a "paddling" as my parents called it, when we arrived home, and I could feel my backside growing warm from just the thought of it. Tears pricked my eyes as I felt a bubble of emotion rise into my throat. I didn't know what I was feeling, so I shoved it into a tight ball of anger.

It never occurred to me that my father's, mother's, and sister's words about me could be anything but true. I took them on and wore their characterizations of what I did and who I was like a cloak. This was the night I accepted that I was both an embarrassment as well as exempt from the category of gifted. The suit fit, and I wore it till the day I died.

My Power

$\mathcal{I}$ knew where I was going. I had scoped out the place months ago and had held it in my memory for the day that, evidently, had arrived. I hadn't known when I would need the services that this place offered me, but I had felt the impending moment sitting just over the horizon for some time, waiting for the right dawn to rise and bring me down with it before the next fall of night. My shoulders felt lightened somehow, and I was on a different kind of high that I had not experienced before. I felt incredibly powerful. My destiny was, without a doubt, in my hands, and I clenched it in my fists fiercely, sucking on the breast of control like a starving infant. At last, I was the one who would make the final call and have the last word. It was the moment I'd been waiting for my whole life, and I was almost drunk from the experience of this long-lived lust finally being satiated.

Despite my mental euphoria, my feet felt heavier with each step, weighing me down increasingly, it seemed, in an effort to stop my advancement altogether. But I continued to push, higher and farther up into the mountainside, growing in both exhaustion and ecstasy.

Finally, in an inextricable combination of triumph and defeat, I arrived at the place where I had visualized my end. A tree with a limb that stretched no more than a foot over the top of my head grew in the midst of the tiniest clearing within the woods of the mountainside. And just beneath the limb, as if it had been placed there just for my convenience, sat a squatty, smooth rock. Nature's very own step stool. I pulled my orange and green climbing rope out from my coat pocket and began to uncoil it, feeling the euphoria I had been enjoying on my climb up the mountain shrivel down into raucous sparks and live wires that seemed to be whipping around lethally in my stomach.

I'd practiced tying a hangman's noose more than a hundred times over the years, using everything from my floss to my shoelaces. However, as soon as I began to form the climbing rope into the shape I thought it should be, my mind went completely blank. I fumbled around for what seemed like hours, working then reworking the loops that, truthfully, were not complex. I grew increasingly angry the longer I struggled, feeling betrayed once again by my body, which was doing its best to preserve a life that I had no interest in continuing to live out.

"Damn you!" I yelled finally, flinging the rope to the ground in fury.

Not even this moment could I get right. The irony of being

so tired of screwing up that I would resort to ending my own life, only to find that even in my attempt to put an end to the failures, I was a failure—that was too much. I sat down on the rock beneath the tree branch and placed my face in my hands. Tears did not come. They had all been spent through the years. Certain seasons had been drier than others, but my tears had all eventually been poured out. Tears, I had realized, were simply a pronouncement of hope—a recognition that there should and could in fact be something better than what is and thus, the expression of sorrow that it is not. My hope was gone and, therefore, so were my tears. I had waited for some sort of validation in moments like this before, sitting with my head in my palms, wishing to be told that I was not as alone as I felt. But no such consolation came. I stood to my feet and picked up the climbing rope that I had thrown to the ground in frustration.

Closing my eyes, I ran my hand over the length of it and took several deep breaths. My anger seemed to subside, and I once again felt the security I had found in my mind being made up return to me. My fingers began to work again and in a short time, my hangman's noose was complete. I stood alone in silence, looking at the work of my hands, until a very still, small voice said, "There is more power in life than in death."

I looked at the tree limb, hanging plaintively just above my head and considered these words. I knew in that moment that I was brave enough to die. What I didn't know was whether I was brave enough to live. I held my noose loosely, swinging it like a pendulum as I contemplated this thought that had just landed on me like a feather or falling leaf. Could it be that, despite how certain I was that this was the ultimate display of my autonomy, a conscious choice to do the opposite of what felt so tantalizingly dominant would in fact be the true demonstration of strength? Slowly, and somewhat angrily, I began to untie my rope, feeling like a part of myself that I did not want to let go of, was dying. I stuffed my rope back into my coat pocket, and with a deep sense of emptiness and defeat, climbed back down the mountain.

Samuel and I
(2020)

Samuel was no more than five when this incident occurred. He sat at our dinner table, working meticulously to string a piece of uncooked macaroni onto a strand of purple yarn that I had cut for him from our basket of knitting supplies. The floor and table were littered with painted wooden beads and assorted noodles of the type that featured a hole for a string to poke through—penne, rigatoni, and the aforementioned macaroni, to name a few.

I stood by the stove, slowly stirring a pot of boiling water and sweet potatoes with a wooden spoon, humming along to Enya as she chanted in the background. I had been impressed with the attention to detail that Samuel had put into each piece that he threaded onto what looked to be the size of a bracelet. He had a small Styrofoam plate by his elbow that was dotted with purple, orange, yellow, blue, and green paint. After selecting a noodle, Sam would pick up his small, well-worn paint brush, and delicately dip it into the desired paint color. With the concentration one would expect of a young surgeon, Samuel would apply the paint, taking great care with each stroke, not to get his fingers messy or spread the color to parts of the shell that he did not want it on. He had requested I supply the noodles, paint, beads, and yarn about an hour ago, and he had been working quietly and diligently since then. Sam was a creative, thoughtful, and fun-loving kid. He never shied away from an adventure but was also willing to sit in quiet and look at a book about birds or spin a Rubik's cube between his fingers.

As I sat marveling at his patience and attention to detail, Sam's baby sister, Amelia, came crawling around the corner of the kitchen island. Up to this point, she had been contentedly playing with a pile of Tupperware that she had pulled out of the bottom cabinets. Her attention was now drawn to the intriguing spread of beads and uncooked pasta that littered the floor. I moved away from my boiling pot and began to systematically collect the dropped choking hazards, starting with those closest to her curious hands and working my way back. Sam did not seem to notice and continued his work on the homemade jewelry. I also continued my work until I heard the hissing of water evaporating off the stove's burner. My pot was boiling over.

"Sam," I said, standing up and rushing to remove the pot from the heat, "will you please finish picking up the beads and noodles off the floor?"

Sam did not seem to hear me. If he did, he did not respond.

"Sam," I said again, becoming agitated at his selective hearing. "Stop what you're doing and pick up all the stuff you've dropped on the floor, please."

Sam's fingers didn't stop moving, but this time, he responded by mumbling, "I don't want to right now."

Had it been the first time that Samuel had refused to listen to a simple request, I may not have reacted to him as strongly as I did. However, the history of power struggles that he and I shared caused this tiny statement to make my face hot and my palms clench.

"Samuel!" My voice was beginning to rise in volume, and I felt the control I once had over my emotions begin to slip. "I didn't ask if it was what you wanted. You are responsible for making this mess, and now you are responsible for cleaning it up!"

Samuel's eyes rolled to the back of his head, and he let out a giant exhale. He was clearly annoyed to pause his work, but he climbed down from his kitchen chair, still holding the precious noodle bracelet in one hand, and began picking up the debris of his project with the other. I returned to my potatoes, satisfied with what seemed like a victory that had not escalated to a screaming match. I tapped my wooden spoon on the edge of the pot and turned around to retrieve a colander to strain the hot water through. As I did so, out of the corner of my eye, I see Amelia reach up with her tiny hand and grab ahold of the end of Samuel's unfinished bracelet. She gives it a determined tug, and in an instant, the noodles and beads are scattered across the floor. Samuel stares in disbelief for a moment. I see his eyes squeeze shut, his face grow red, and his small hands ball up into fists. I open my mouth to say something in an effort to comfort and calm him, but before a word can leave my mouth, one of those small, balled fists lands squarely on the nose of little Amelia, who at that moment, had been intently studying a purple and green rigatoni that had landed between her hands.

The calm and comforting words immediately evaporated from my tongue, and I screamed, "No!" slamming the pot of potatoes and colander down. I crossed the kitchen in one giant step and snatched Samuel's arm as roughly as I could. I wanted to inflict pain. "You **never** hit your little sister."

Sam looked up at me in defiance. His bottom lip was quivering with emotion while tears built behind his eyes, but his brow remained furrowed, his face straining to remain contorted into one that was full of defiance. He would not break to show fear or sorrow.

He said nothing, so I continued my rant. "She is smaller than you! I don't care what she does, you never use your body to hurt her!"

Samuel bent down and began to pick up his precious noodles and beads that had been scattered everywhere. His refusal to acknowledge what I just said or show any shame or remorse for what he had just done to his sister caused something inside me to snap.

I zeroed in on the orange piece of penne that Sam's hands were moving toward, and I stomped on it. The noodle was crushed beneath my weight. Sam froze, his arm still extended toward the now shattered penne. I didn't stop but begin to crush every piece of painted pasta I saw within my leg's reach.

"No, stop!" Samuel cries, tears streaming down his face. He grabbed my shirt and pulled at it, begging me to cease in my destruction of his creation. "Please, don't!" he screamed. "Please!"

But I did not listen. I sought out every piece of noodle that showed any marking of the time or love that had been invested in it by my son, and I crushed it.

Abigail and I
(2000)

My mother Abigail always seemed to stay busy. She would walk from one room to the next as if there was a fire that needed to be put out: living room, kitchen, bedroom, bathroom, kitchen, bathroom, living room, bedroom, bathroom. As a child, I would try to keep up with her location. Perhaps we are all born with that instinct to know the fastest route to access the person or thing that should offer and serve as our safe place. I sat on our old burgundy couch holding a children's book about a giraffe and his rapidly melting ice cream, but all my attention was on my mother. I had been waiting all morning for her to take a break in her unending to-ing and fro-ing from room to room. Abigail carried a mop out of the bathroom and leaned it up against the wall; then she walked to the back bedroom while wiping her hands on the back of her blue jeans. She emerged shortly after, carrying my brother's bedspread and an armful of blankets. I watched patiently as she walked outside the house and onto the porch. I heard her shaking them vigorously and then the soft flapping sound of the heavy fabric being draped carefully over the railing. The door opened and closed again, and my mom reentered the room. She seemed to pause, her mind ticking through a mental checklist. I held my breath, hoping that this is it. Her eyes flick toward the kitchen as if a light bulb had gone off, and she turned her back to me and walked to the sink. She lifted a bowl full of soaking dish rags out of its basin and returned to the porch where she wrung each one out before placing them along the railing to dry. Once again, the front door opened and shut and my mom stood next to me by the couch, never once noticing me or my eyes that had been glued to her for the past several hours.

Her body seemed to relax for a split-second. I took that moment and asked, "Momma, will you read me this book?" Instantly, her relaxed frame stiffened, and she snapped her head around to meet my hopeful gaze.

"Child!" my body responded with relief at the sound of my mother's attention directed toward me for the first time that day and recoiled at the harsh edge with which it was spoken. "Have you not seen how busy I've been all morning?" she asked.

I had indeed. Since before I had awakened, my mother had been scurrying throughout the house, washing dishes, stripping beds, scrubbing windows, mopping floors, folding laundry, beating cushions, and cleaning mirrors. This was a normal routine in our home.

I did not interrupt my mother's assault on the dirt and disorder of her house. I knew better than that. Instead, as usual, I had walked to the kitchen to prepare my own breakfast. I had dragged a chair across the floor to the cabinet to fetch myself a bowl. I had then hopped down, placed my bowl on the chair, and pushed them both to the other side of the kitchen where I was able to retrieve a box of cereal. I had poured myself some cereal, taking great care to get each flake and nugget into the porcelain bowl without dropping any onto the floor. I carefully folded down the plastic bag inside the box when I was done and neatly closed the folding lid of the cardboard shut before placing it back into the cabinet. Grabbing the milk from the fridge proved to be a difficult task as it was a freshly opened gallon jug, but I had been successful, nonetheless.

It was for this reason, however, that my efforts to pour the milk into my bowl without spilling resulted in a clumsy struggle and a small pool of milk that encircled my cereal bowl. I immediately felt a lump form in my throat, and butterflies of the worst type began to flutter around my stomach. I searched around the kitchen frantically, looking for a rag to clean it up with. The drawer full of kitchen towels had been neatly folded with freshly laundered cloths that I dared not make the wrong selection from. I knew that there were dishrags and decorative kitchen towels, but I did not know which was which. I also knew that making the mistake of using a decorative towel to clean up spilled milk would be worse than spilling the milk in the first place. The sink was spotless, and my mother had already hauled off the cleaning tools she had used that morning to be washed. I began to panic, knowing that soon my mother would come around the corner and find the mess I had made.

Finally, I peeled off my pajama shirt and placed it over the spill, allowing the flannel to soak up the milk. I pushed my chair up to the side of the sink and then, after climbing up, carefully ran warm water over the soiled pajamas. I wrung my shirt out as best as I could, then carried it outside to hang it up to dry. I returned to my breakfast, feeling proud of my problem-solving abilities and had just sat down with my spoon when I heard my mother's exasperated exhale. I looked up to see her staring in frustration at a trail of water droplets that ran from the sink to the front door.

"Five minutes?" she said, looking at the floor in disgust. "Five minutes, you're out of bed, and already, you've created a mess on the floors that I've spent all morning mopping." I looked down at my cereal feeling waves of shame, guilt, and disgust at my own inability to do anything right as they wash from my forehead down to my toes. This had been the only time my mother interacted with me that morning.

She glared at me, the source of all the dirt and disorder, the reason for her war. Her enemy. "I haven't sat down all day or had a minute for just myself!" she continued. "Can you not just give me some air—some time to just breathe once I finally finish cleaning up *your* mess? You jump on me the second I'm done. I'm tired . . ." she said, her voice trailing off as she walked away from me to the back room.

I sat alone on the couch and for the first time, I looked down at the book. The disappointment I had anticipated finally fell on me like a heavy blanket. I shoved the book out of my lap and buried my face in the couch—the spot that had, over the years, slowly become my safe place.

Abigail and Donna
(1970)

*A*bigail sat rigidly at her desk, gripping her pencil between her index finger and thumb as tightly as she could. Her mouth worked a piece of chewing gum intensely, pausing only now and then to blow a bubble, and her eyes were so focused on the small piece of paper in front of her that they were almost crossed. "Aaa . . ." she whispered to herself. "Beeh . . ." her fingers grew white at the tips as she strained to control her pencil. "Guuh . . ."

"Shut up!" the girl at the desk in front of Abigail's snapped.

Abigail didn't move her eyes away from her paper, but she shut her mouth and returned to her intense gum chewing, trying to maintain her concentration on her writing.

She finished her final letter and leaned back with a sigh of satisfaction, picking up her paper and smiling admiringly at the work she had just completed. Her own name, written in a scrawling cursive hand. Abigail raised her hand and waved it excitedly at the front of the classroom.

"Miss Donna!" she called, "I'm finished!" A tall woman looked up over her glasses.

"Very good, Miss Abi. Now write it a few mo' times."

Abigail looked down at her page, proud of the work she had completed, but daunted by the task of replicating it. She took a deep breath and picked up her pencil again. Resuming her posture of utter engrossment, Abigail began to write her name a second time.

"Aaah . . ." she said again.

"I said shut up!" the girl in front of her hissed, whirling around in her seat.

Abigail looked up this time and retorted, "It helps me concentrate!"

"Well, I don't care! It's distracting me," she said, before turning away and resuming her own writing.

Abigail wrinkled her nose in frustration and then, with great enthusiasm continued, "Beeeeeh . . ."

Immediately, the girl in front of her whipped around and snatched the piece of paper from under her pencil. Before Abigail could stop her, the girl ripped the paper in half and threw it on the floor.

Abigail stared at the floor in disbelief for a moment before the girl said, "And stop blowing bubbles with your stupid chewing gum."

Without thinking, Abigail reached her hand into her mouth and lunged forward. Grabbing a hunk of the girl's curly hair, Abigail pulled apart her pink, sticky gum and wadded it into the girl's ringlets. Shrieking, the girl pulled away, clawing at her bird's nested hair.

"Miss Donna! Miss Donna! Abigail wadded her gum into my hair!" she hollered.

The woman at the front of the classroom stood up and called both girls to the front, her voice tight and firm. Abigail hung her head and fixed her eyes on the tops of her shoes as Miss Donna inspected her classmate's matted hair.

After a moment, Miss Donna took a sharp inhale and said, "Well, looks like it's in there." She paused to pull a pair of scissors out of her top desk drawer. "Not much I can do."

The girl with the gum in her hair yelped and jumped away at the sight of the small silver blades. "Nooo," she sobbed, tugging at her sticky curls. "Please, don't cut my hair!" she pleaded.

Miss Donna just shook her head, "Ain't much else you can do with it, child," she said, gesturing to her desk chair. Whimpering, the girl took a seat, burying her face in her hands as Miss Donna snipped her thick brown locks off.

Abigail stood silently, gripping her own braid with both hands, as she watched in wide-eyed horror at the consequence of what she had done. When Miss Donna was finished, she tapped the girl on the shoulder and motioned for her to go back to her desk. Solemnly, with hair cut to the bottom of her ears and a tear-soaked shirt, the little girl rose to her feet and made her way to the back of the room without a sound. Abigail turned to follow her when Miss Donna stopped her.

"Miss Abi, where you goin'?"

Abigail swallowed hard, confused, and scared. "I . . . I was just goin' to go back to my desk, Miss Donna."

"And why," Miss Donna asks, crossing her arms, "should you keep your hair on your head when you are the reason that lil Miss Becky had to have hers chopped off?"

Abigail's hands fly again to her long braid. "No," she whispered, tears beginning to well up in her eyes. "Please, please don't cut my hair, Miss Donna."

Miss Donna said nothing, but with a stern gaze, gestured toward the chair, still scattered with Becky's sticky clumps of ringlets. Abigail began to sob, moving her feet that felt like they were made of lead. She sat down, feeling panic and shame well up explosively inside her chest. Miss Donna picked up her scissors, and slowly, without much thought, began to chop off the top of Abi's long golden braid. Before she had even finished, Abigail burst into uncontrolled tears.

"You people care too much about appearances," she heard Miss Donna mutter to herself. She finished the final snip, then dropped the detached braid into Abigail's lap. "And let this remind ya, Miss Abigail, to keep yo' mess out of other people's hair."

Donna and Oscar
(1940)

*D*onna was trying to keep her mouth from opening. What might come out, should she dare let her lips part—whether an angry scream or a terrified wail— would only escalate the already seemingly precarious situation. Both her parents stood calmly, their eyes cast toward the floor, averted from the condescending glare of the man in the uniform. The only sign that her father was in any way phased by the situation that her family found themselves in, was the whitened knuckles that peeked out of the side of his jacket's pocket. Her mother, holding her swollen belly with one hand, and gripping the bicep of her husband with the other, looked as blank-faced as a dead woman. Neither of her parent's dared show any sign of emotion, so neither did Donna.

"You comprehend the serious profundity of this situation,

don't ya boy?" the man in the uniform inquired. The way he spoke to her father made Donna think he didn't really care about, or even want a response. Her father must have picked up on the same cues because he remained motionless and quiet. The officer flicked the tip of her dad's hat and got up real close so that their noses were almost touching. "He don't seem like he's been raised right. Don't you know how to train a boy, boy?" Donna wished the man in the uniform would stop calling her dad, 'boy.' Something about the way he said it made her feel a mix of anger and shame, two emotions she couldn't reconcile. Was this man wrong for treating her dad this way, or was there a valid reason behind why she felt this embarrassment?

Before Donna was able to settle these thoughts, her older brother and another man in a uniform came around the side of the car. "Okay, Oscar?" the other officer asked. The man standing before her parents nodded, never taking his eyes away from her father's. He did a slow roll of the tongue then spat something brown and slimy out of his mouth and onto her dad's shoe. Her brother had his hands behind his back, as if they were stuck in his pant pockets. Donna heard him mumble under his breath, "did'n do nothin'." And then, as if lightening had struck, everything happened before Donna knew what had happened. Oscar whipped his neck around, a vein popping out of its side. "What you say, nigger?" For the first time, her mother opened her mouth and, half demanding, half pleading, said, "Keep quiet, Henry."

"No," the officer's neck snapped back around to face her mother, "you keep quiet, bitch. I wasn't talkin' to you."

And he gave her mother a shove. She took one step back and caught her footing.

This time, her dad opened his mouth. Donna was surprised by how calm her dad's voice remained, but she detected a small tremor at the end of each word. "Yessuh. Thank you, suh. She did'n mean no disrespect."

But then, her mother spoke again, and this time, her voice was no longer calm. "I am pregnant!" she cried. "Don't go shovin' on me!"

Oscar's face turned stony, and without hesitation, he grabbed Donna's mother by the shoulder, and forced her to her knees, then stomach. Putting his full weight onto her back, the officer spat into her ear, as he leaned his face close to hers, "You think I care about a nigger baby?"

Then in one swift motion, he stood up and forcefully kicked the woman in her abdomen. Donna's mother began to weep. Whether it was from the pain that the officer's boot had inflicted or from the crippling feeling that Donna herself was experiencing, of being at the mercy of cruel, unjust men, Donna didn't know.

But the flurry of movement that happened after that act of violence, once again, brought her out of her efforts to make sense of what she had just witnessed. The peripheral sight of two figures struggling, followed by two gunshots, left Donna with a ringing in her ears, and without a father.

Oscar and Bart
(1920)

Oscar sat by the side of the road, watching the dust settle after it was stirred up in the wake of the cars that occasionally drove by. He held a forked stick in one of his pudgy hands and used it to poke at the dry, yellow grass that clumped up in random patches around where he was perched. He did this every afternoon. The sun would start almost directly over his dusty red head, and every day, it would set before he ever saw the headlights of Bart's Willys truck come bumping down the terracotta road.

Bart was Oscar's father or so Oscar had been told. He didn't know the man much, for they rarely spent time together. Miss Alma, the neighbor lady, would sit with him for a few hours almost every day, and she always brought a treat for them to share. Whether it was some fresh squeezed lemonade or a chunk of cornbread with a schmear of butter on top, Oscar would look forward to and anticipate her company, almost as much as he did his father's return home. It was, Oscar had learned, his only opportunity to get any time or attention from his father. The truck would pull into the prickly plot of earth in front of their shanty, and for a moment, if his dad was in a good mood, Oscar would make eye contact with him and feel his father's hand on his head as he brushed his rough fingers over the top of his hair. If not, the two would walk side by side to the front door where Oscar would eagerly swing it open to let his dad enter—an act that would, on occasion, garner a curt nod of gratitude or even a, "Thank ya."

Oscar, growing tired of his game of poke-the-grass-with-the-stick, cocked his arm back and let the branch go flying across the road, just as Miss Alma emerged from her hut. "What an ahm!" she hollered. "You needa be playin' ball wid a throw like dat."

Oscar felt his ears grow warm and red from her praise. "Thank ya, Miss Alma," he mumbled, too embarrassed to raise his voice to match her enthusiasm.

"Well, lucky I brought us uh meal fo' champ-yuns," she said, setting a plate down.

It was covered with a green gingham cloth that she waved and whirled her hands over as if she was a magician about to perform a magic trick. Then, with that same theatrical flair, she picked up its corner and pulled it off to reveal two fudgey brownies. "They thuh new thing," she said proudly, scooching the plate a little closer to Oscar to make room for herself next to him on his plot of dirt. "One bite o' those," she said, "and you'll have all yuh need tuh hit a home run."

Miss Alma selected the fatter of the two brownies and offered it to him. Oscar took it and held it carefully between his thumb and pointer finger, unsure of what to expect of something that looked so decadent. He took a peek at Miss Alma out of the corner of his eye, and she smiled and nodded encouragingly. "Don't stew, baby," she coaxed, "it won't be a love you make'n lose in one day. I'll make ya mo' iffn you take to um."

Oscar returned his gaze to the brownie and was about to take his first bite when he heard the familiar sound of his dad's Willys truck. The sun was still high and, though Oscar always found himself waiting for his father's return hours before he arrived, he was quite surprised that his dad would make his appearance before sundown. Miss Alma looked up too, noticing the change in Oscar's attention, and patted his shoulder.

"There now," said Miss Alma. "A whole afternoon early. My, my, my, what a treat."

Oscar felt a small flutter of excitement enter his body at the possibilities that suddenly presented themselves. His father would be home a whole afternoon early, like Miss Alma had said, and what was there to do? They could go fishin' or coonin' or maybe even go to town. Oscar tried to calm his small body down, but he felt his feet getting dancy and his hands getting fidgety. As the sound of the truck drew closer, Oscar noticed that the speed of its approach was faster than usual. Oscar strained his eyes toward the end of the road, just as the old black truck came into view. It came roaring across the dry earth in a sloppy zigzag, throwing clouds of red dust into the air. Oscar felt Miss Alma stiffen by his side, and he looked up at her questioningly.

She did not take her eyes off the swerving truck, but said in a calm, firm voice, "Baby, let's back off o' this side o' duh road." Oscar looked back at the truck that was quickly approaching. Bart seemed to be in a hurry and in that moment, Oscar felt panic at the possibility of losing his opportunity to spend time with his father, should he move away from his waiting place.

"Baby," Miss Alma said, her voice sounding urgent. "C'mon now; let's move ovah." Oscar began to wring his hands anxiously.

"But Miss Alma . . . ," he started to protest.

Before he was able to complete his sentence, Miss Alma yanked him up by his arm and tossed his whole body into the air and across the yellow pokey grass. There was a tremendous bang and then the hiss of steam being released. Oscar scrambled to his feet, bewildered at what had just happened. His dad's Willys truck sat crumpled against the embankment where he and Miss Alma had just been sitting.

Bart stumbled out of the cab, gripping an amber bottle in one fist and trying repeatedly to slam the door of the truck shut with the other. "Dammit," Bart mumbled, surveying the damage of his recklessness. "Least weren't nothin' but a blacky," he muttered, taking one long swig from his bottle before throwing the empty glass into the grass. It made a hollow thud and rolled til, *'clink,'* it met the edge of a porcelain plate holding one fudge brownie. Oscar stared at the plate hard. He didn't want to look at what lay next to it, beneath the wheels of his dad's smoking truck.

"D-Dad?" Oscar asked, not taking his eyes off the brownie, "can . . . can we go fishin'?"

Bart and Martha
(1890)

*B*art straddled an old, mossy log, swinging his left foot rhythmically over the surface of the water that flowed beneath his nature-made perch. Every so often, he would pull an acorn or smooth rock that he'd collected along his path to the river from his trouser pants and flip it into the moving water like tossing a coin into a wishing well. A bird whistled overhead, and he returned the call cheerily. The day seemed perfect beneath the protection of the tree's canopy of limbs. To Bart, the limbs felt like a mother bird's wing, stretching over him in a protective stance of defense, safeguarding and preserving their cherished one. Here, by the rushing river and sweet melody of the wild, was where Bart felt most at home.

A rustle in the brush across from Bart drew his attention from the sound of bird song, and he rose from his seat to investigate. A pitiful bleat and more rustling reached his ears in the same moment that Bart laid his eyes upon a small black and white goat kid. Its right hind quarter was wedged between two large rocks and twisted in an unnatural way in relation to the rest of its body. The little goat lay on its side exhausted, mustering enough energy only to cry out for help and shuffle its hooves.

"Oh, fella!" Bart dropped to his knees and slowly extended one hand to the goat's small black and white speckled head while reaching to move one of the rocks away with his other. The goat's eyes grow wide, and it began to bleat faster and louder in fear, kicking its three free legs in protest at the approach of a stranger.

"Hey, hey; it's okay, fella," Bart said soothingly, rubbing the goat's forehead with his thumb. "I won't hurt ya. I want to help ya. I like to help. Can I help?"

The goat's eyes remained wild, its small body heaving air rapidly through its nostrils in distress. But it stopped fighting with its legs and lay still, surrendering to Bart's approach.

"There . . ." he continued, rubbing the backs of the goat's ears, as he slowly began to work the smaller of the two large rocks to the side, taking great care not to farther exacerbate the stress being put on the goat's hind leg. "We can fix this together," he said softly.

The moment the leg was loose, the small goat endeavored to rise on its hooves to flee. It immediately stumbled over its crippled leg and collapsed into the dirt.

"Oh, friend, you've broken your leg for certain," Bart said, taking a step toward the goat. Again, the kid attempted to run away and again, it crumpled from its injury. "Come on, friend," he whispered, scooping the goat's small form into his arms. "I won't hurt ya. I can still help ya. Let me help ya," he said, rising to his feet.

The two set off down the path that Bart took to reach his place by the river, and after a few moments, the goat calmed and dozed off into a peaceful slumber, cradled in Bart's arms. "It's nice to know you, friend," Bart said, smiling down at the closed eyes of the small kid he had just rescued. "Can I call you that?" he asked. "Can I call you friend?"

The goat let out a satisfied exhale of approval, and Bart beamed with joy over the new companion he has found. Bart's mother stood outside by their laundry line as he emerged from the woods, still holding "Friend" in his arms.

"Bartholomew, whatcha got there?" she calls.

Bart picked up his feet in anticipation, eager to introduce Friend to his mother. "This fella got his hind quarter stuck by the river. I helped him, ma," he panted.

Bart's mother, Martha, smiled down at him and the snoozing kid. "That's nice, baby. I'm glad you could help. Now, will you help *me* collect the rest of this laundry?" she asked.

Bart nodded and carefully placed Friend down on a particularly cushy looking patch of green grass before doing his part to help his mother with her chores. Bart spent the next several weeks with Friend, carrying him outside regularly, so he wouldn't soil the house, feeding him with a cloth dipped in milk, and stroking his side to help him sleep. Friend's leg healed thanks to Bart's attention and care, and the goat quickly became Bart's shadow, following him everywhere he went.

One morning, after Friend had grown from a kid to a large, healthy goat, Martha called Bart into the back of the cabin where she stood over the wood stove heating a pot of water. "I'm mighty proud of you, Bart," she said, smiling. "You did a good job growing that goat up."

Bart smiled brightly at his mother's praise. "He's about big enough for us to benefit from all that hard work now," she said, wiping her hands on her apron and turning from her pot of water.

Bart looked at his mother quizzically. "Okay, Ma, but I don't think boy goats can give milk."

Martha laughed heartily and tousled Bart's hair. "You always know how to make me laugh, darlin'," she said. "You are certainly right. We can't get milk from 'im, but we can get a really fine goat stew."

Bart's face paled, and he felt panic erupt in his belly like a dam that just burst. "M-Ma," Bart stammered, incredulous at her suggestion. "You don't mean you wanna kill, Friend, do ya?" he asks.

Martha smiled kindly. "Oh, honey, we can't keep animals as pets. They gotta serve us a purpose. I don't *want* to kill your goat. But we need food and can't afford to house animals that don't contribute to our livelihood."

"He serves a purpose!" Bart protested. "He's my friend! My only friend, Ma! Please don't take him from me, Ma!"

Tears began to well up behind Bart's eyes at the thought of losing Friend. Martha shook her head and turned away. "You can't survive in this world being so soft," his mother said sharply. "The world ain't kind. If you waste your energy protecting small creatures instead of caring for yourself, you won't survive."

Martha opened a drawer and took out a sharp knife. "You need to learn to silence those feelings that make you weak," she said, handing him the blade. "Like I said, you can't survive if you have feelings for small things that don't matter."

Bart looked up at her, pleading with his eyes. "Small things that don't matter?" he asked. "Ma, how can you say Friend don't matter?"

Martha's eyes narrowed, and her voice rose in anger. "Because he don't!" she said flatly. "Things that are fragile and weak don't matter! Now go. Bring me back the meat once you've cleaned it. We'll have the stew tonight."

Bart looked down at the blade, frozen in dread and fear. "Ma . . ." Bart's voice broke.

"Go!" Martha yelled. "You need to learn this lesson *now*."

Bart stumbled out the door, holding the knife loosely, his body trembling. As soon as Bart emerged from the cabin, Friend danced up to his side, bleating joyfully at the sight of his savior.

Martha and Eric
(1850)

Martha sat on top of a coiled rope, her legs dangling freely just above the rough, wet wood of the ship's deck. She had become attuned to the rhythm of the pitch and rise of the bow. With every dip into the trough of the waves, came a sudden drop in her stomach. It signaled to her brain to squeeze her eyes shut in anticipation of the ocean spray on her face that came directly after, as the boat rose to meet the crest of the sea's dance. This was her favorite place on the ship. Though wet and often cold, it was also peaceful and always beautiful. The horizon offered her hope that she could not fully understand in her small heart, but it continued to pull her back to this same place on the deck of this ship that was carrying her family and her to America. Martha pulled her faded cloth doll to her chest and inhaled deeply as she watched a group of young boys who stood a stone's throw away from her playing with their painted wooden tops.

"Ahoy there, Miss."

Martha looked up to meet the gaze of Eric, an old sailor she'd befriended during her time up on deck. Eric had dark, leathery skin, wrinkled from his long days spent working beneath the sun over the ocean. He first noticed her several weeks ago, sitting in her preferred haven on top of the coiled rope. After introducing himself, Eric made a point of saying hello to Martha and sharing brief conversations with her in passing as he went about his work on the ship. Occasion- ally, Eric even went to the trouble of smuggling some of the treats that had been brought aboard solely for the captain's enjoyment. Small chunks of bread with a schmear of but- ter, canned milk, and even on occasion a slice of sugar cake, would be snuck from the larder and brought directly to her by Eric's design. She smiled up at the face of her new friend.

"Hello, Mister Eric!" she said, shading her eyes from the sun. Eric took a step forward, blocking its rays with his large frame and casting a shadow over Martha's small form. Blushing, Martha lowered her hand and looked down, fum- bling with her doll. She suddenly felt uneasy with how close Eric was standing to her.

"Fine day for a rope sitting," Eric said approvingly. "Mighty fine." Eric placed his hands on his lower back and leaned into them, giving his chest a big stretch. "But Miss," Eric redi- rected, "I've got an even finer idea of something to do."

Martha's eyes brightened at the thought of a new way to

pass the time. It had been several days since she had felt truly engrossed in anything of true entertainment or enjoyment, having spent most of her time just staring into the horizon toward which they sailed.

Eric motioned with a large, worn hand toward a pile of heavy, wooden crates that were stacked higher than the top of his head. "I'll show you what I'm talking about just over here . . . ," he said, moving toward them as he waved her over in a welcoming gesture.

Martha hopped off her rope, still clutching her doll. Her heart was beating wildly with curiosity and something else that she didn't fully understand. Eric waited for her to walk past him, ushering her around the corner of the edge of the crates. Once she rounded it, she saw that there was nothing there but a few barrels, and what looked to be a torn sail, laying on the deck. She turned quizzically to Eric, but he now had his back to her, busily dragging and stacking barrels. It was then that she noticed they were walled in on every side by the crates, with the only entry to their alcove currently being blockaded by her friend.

Martha felt her stomach begin to tighten into an uncomfortable ball. Her curiosity, now gone, was replaced with a feeling of being trapped and vulnerable. "Mister Eric . . ." she began, but then stopped abruptly as he turned back toward her, his face shaped into a look that she had not seen before.

"Oh, " he sighed, as if he had just relieved himself of something, "I love it when you call me Mister."

Martha's mouth went dry. Her hands stopped fumbling

with her doll, and she became a statue, gripping the blue cloth so hard her knuckles turned white. She didn't understand what was happening, but she was terrified. Eric's eyes looked like he wanted to devour her, and she shrank from them. Eric took a step forward, and Martha instinctively withdrew. "No where to go, Miss." he said smoothly. "It's just us, and I want to show you some fun things we can do on this fine day."

Martha wanted to cry, but she bit her lip, somehow feeling that to shed a tear would be a loss for her. Eric took another step toward her and motioned to her sun faded dress. "Take that off," he said flatly, as if he had just told her that her shoe was untied. Martha's eyes widened, and she felt her face blush again. She hesitated long enough that Eric began to move forward again, this time with an intensity that frightened her. Immediately, she dropped her doll and began to clumsily unfasten the buttons that ran down the length of her dress. Eric smiled wryly, "Remember," he glowered, "this can be fun."

Martha's whole body began to shake as, one at a time, she slipped the sleeves of her dress off her shoulders and stood naked and exposed to the hungry eyes of the now, cruel-looking face of someone she once trusted. The shame and fear she felt did not allow her to look up, but she heard the rustling of Eric's britches and then the clank of his belt buckle hit the deck. Martha heard Eric's boots step one by one out of his pant legs, then step 1, 2, 3, 4, 5, toward her. His rough hand grabbed her by the waist, and she felt her body being pushed to the wet, hard, wooden surface of the deck. The smell of salt and mold filled her nose and mouth before it was covered by that of Eric's stale taste of rum. Martha, unable to keep her tears back, began to convulse in heaving sobs.

"Hush, Miss," warned Eric. "It ain't your fault you're small and weak. But this is how the world is for people like you. Best not go against nature."

Eric and Thomas
(1800)

Eric sat on a mossy, damp stone beneath a bridge, his chin resting on his hands and his arms propped up by his knees. The clouds overhead took turns blocking out any light that might seek to shine its rays upon the people in the city below. The persistent drip of rainwater running off from the street that crossed over the top of the bridge kept the puddles surrounding Eric's feet full and disturbed, sending rippling rings from the center to the perimeter of the collected water in an unending cycle. Eric's father, Thomas, stood by his side, his hands in his pant pockets, his eyes cast to the cobblestone beneath his feet.

Eric did not know why his father had brought him here, but his mother's tearful farewell to them prior to their departure into the city had frightened him. Each evening with his parents had grown increasingly difficult. He and his younger brothers and sisters had learned at an early age to make minimal noise, contribute to the family's resources in whatever capacity they could, and keep their expectations low for any physical needs that they may have. Hungry, cold, and sleepless nights were what the children had grown accustomed to. It was a rare occasion that Eric fell asleep without a biting pang of emptiness in his stomach and a chilling wind on his back. Yet despite his unmet needs, Eric's family still struggled to care for the rest of their brood.

Eric's father would often say to him, "You've survived this long without," as he would scoop one of the small chunks of potato his mother had given him at dinner and place it on the plate of one of his younger brothers and sisters who was sick or weakened. He had grown resilient from the lack of attention that his parents afforded him, and he shouldered the task of derelict as a soldier would a posting. Nevertheless, Eric was, as his parents had voiced the night before, "one mouth too many." He had fought hard to keep his ears closed to the harsh and disparaging voices of his parents that had floated toward him where he had lain that night, pretending to be asleep. But despite his effort to distract and ignore, he had heard and understood his parents' opinion of him and his place in the family. He was a burden. Now as he sat beneath this stone bridge with his father, waiting for he knew not what, Eric felt small, but not small enough.

"Thomas," a gruff voice from behind the father and son penetrated the thick silence that lay between them and they, in unison, turned their heads. A rough looking sailor with a patchy beard and dark, worn skin approached them, his gait off-kilter, and his expression hard.

"Willy," Eric's father directed a short nod of acknowledgement, keeping his eyes averted from Eric who was seeking them in question.

"Hrrrm," Willy grunted, glancing over Eric in a way that made him feel less valuable than the roaches scurrying underfoot. "You say he's strong?" Willy asked, doubtfully.

Thomas cleared his throat and without much emotion replied, "He can do a lot. Though I know he don't look like it."

Willy nodded slowly, still looking Eric up and down. "How old you say? Twelve?"

"Eleven, actually," Thomas said, his eyes still studying the cobblestone.

Willy grunted again and pulled a leather pouch from the pocket of his trousers. Eric saw him pull a few coins from it and slip them back into his pants; then Willy tossed the pouch at his father's chest, sending a dozen coins tinkling onto the cobblestone.

"He ain't what you said he was," Willy said roughly, "but I'll take 'im any way." Willy gripped Eric by the shoulder and said, "Up, lad," then strode off, out from under the bridge into the drizzling rain. Eric looked again to his father, hoping for an explanation or at least a final chance to lock eyes with him, but Thomas was busy picking up the dropped coins. With his hands in his pockets and an emptiness in his body that he somehow had not yet felt before, Eric walked out into the rain, following Willy to wherever he was leading.

Thomas and Alice
(1760)

Thomas leaned against the mahogany carved encasement of a large window seat in his family's drawing room. Rain splattered against the panes, blurring the vision of the outdoors. All he could see was a wash of green and gray, a dim reflection of the sprawling fields that surrounded his family's estate. A clock ticked on the mantel next to him, agitating his senses in contrast to the silence within the rest of the house. Many moments had passed Thomas by on this perch.

Though perhaps not in conscious thought, he returned to his hiding place often in hopes of being missed by those from whom he had withdrawn. A door to the home opened and closed, and Thomas heard footsteps approach.

"There you are! Come, come. I've been out for the better half of the morning, and I am in need of your company now."

His mother Alice's face, prettily painted and always affixed with a pleasant disposition, appeared at the entrance of the drawing room just long enough to summon her son. As quickly as she had appeared, she vanished from the hall, on her way to the next matter of concern, trusting her son was obediently trailing behind. "I was in town this morning," she continued as she floated down a set of a stairs, her gloved hand gliding on the banister like a swan through a quiet lake.

Thomas followed awkwardly, trying to keep a distance that would allow him to both hear the words his mother spoke with her back to him, while also taking care not to tread on the hem of her dress. "And I had the pleasure and good fortune to encounter Mrs. Beall and her son, August. You remember August, don't you dear?"

Thomas parted his lips to affirm his mother's presumption, but she continued, evidently not desiring a response to her inquiry. "She and Mr. Beall have been doing well for themselves, it seems. I admit that I was quite impressed with her upon our meeting. And August has grown, as one might expect. Indeed, you are quite close in age, are you not? I should not have been half so surprised as I was, I should say, given I've seen my very own son grow just as much all this time, but my," she exclaimed, whirling about to face Thomas, "it took the breath out of me!"

Thomas nodded his understanding and smiled, eager to serve as good company. Alice's disposition seemed to shift the next moment, her wide and excited eyes calming and her tone of voice lowering. She sat down on a peach-colored satin lounge and patted the seat next to her. "Mrs. Beall," she continued slowly, "told me about this marvelous opportunity that she and Mr. Beall have prepared for August."

She paused, watching Thomas's face. He continued to look at his mother attentively, patiently waiting for the continuation of her story, and so she pressed on. "Have you ever," she asked, watching Thomas's face intently, "heard of the University of Halle?"

Thomas shook his head, his brows beginning to furrow quizzically.

"Oh! It is marvelous from what I hear!" The enthusiasm his mother had shown from the moment she returned home reemerged as she began to convey to Thomas all that she had learned about Halle from Mrs. Beall. "It is, to my understanding, the center of Pietism in Europe. Truly, the city on a hill, my dear. And you," she said, touching a gloved hand softly to Thomas's cheek, "could be a part of that prestigious, devout work."

Thomas cleared his throat, biding time before a response was expected of him. "Mother," he began, now attuning to Alice's facial expressions as she had to his, "where is this university?"

Alice clapped her hands together and brought them to her pursed lips in excitement. "And that," she announced, her voice rising an octave, "is the very best part!"

Thomas waited, a short silence filling the room with anticipation. "Halle University is in Prussia!" the silence returned to the room, as Thomas sat in stillness, unsure what to say or do in response to his mother's clear enthusiasm.

Sensing his reticence, Alice took both of her son's hands in hers and said confidently, "There is no doubt, my dear, that it was not an accident that I encountered Mrs. Beall today. God has laid this path before you! Halle University is of good status, and you will be acquiring all the knowledge you will need to please God at the very source of piety!" Alice paused and settled back, looking Thomas over with eyes that seemed to be sizing him for a new waistcoat.

"Yes," she said, nodding her head confidently, "I am certain that, should you choose to use your life doing any other work, you will not only fail, but be an incredible disappointment to not just me, but to God."

Alice and Sabrina
(1720)

The brusque sound of a heaving chest, pressing air through narrowed, swollen passages pushed into the air, thrusting, it seemed, peace and hope out the opened windows. No light was in the room, except a single wax candle that dripped pitifully onto the rough, wooden surface of a small table in the corner. Alice sat wrapped in a blanket, moving her gaze back and forth slowly from the glowing light to the tiny form laid out on the bed. Her younger sister Hitty's white gown was splattered with blood and mucus from the draining wounds that covered her underarms and inner thighs, and though the night had laid its dark folds on them like a suppressive blanket of silence, the moments of quiet were split regularly by the sound of Hitty's body fighting for air and clarity.

Alice and Hitty's mother, Sabrina, sat on the bed next to

her young daughter, pressing a soiled, wet cloth against the feverish forehead of her sick child. Tears poured unendingly from the mother's eyes, the grief of loss already descending onto the house that sat among a row of homes that had already seen the slow destruction of eight children under their shelter. From where would their help come? Death had arrived, swinging its sword up and down the roads of Marseille, its hunger unchallenged. And thus darkness entered and feasted mercilessly on all it chose to wrap its fist about. Bodies laid piled up upon carts in the alley waiting to be hauled off to the outskirts of the city with each dawn. Graves large enough to hold hundreds opened up like massive mouths waiting to be filled, their teeth of decomposition and decay fixed to grind away at those they are fed for the years to come.

Hitty, it seemed, had been plucked from the masses as one chosen for consumption, and her final stand against its advances was coming to a close. Her pale, paper thin eyelids fluttered for a moment, as if she was trying to open them. The corners of her cracked, purple lips twitched, a vowel edging on her tongue.

"Dear Hitty," Sabrina whispered, "you may go, my precious child. Go in peace, my darling. I will hold you with me always."

Anguish drenched these last words spoken by a mother as within that moment she felt the tangible reality of her child being ripped from her arms. Indeed, it was as those final words slipped from Sabrina's lips that Hitty's young life also slipped quietly out the window and floated away, following the now cold trail of hope and peace.

Alice stood, dropping her blanket to the cold floor and walked to the edge of the bloody cot, leaning over her baby sister's tiny body.

"Mother," she asked, gazing at the flushed, beautiful face, now devoured by death, "is there a god?"

Sabrina did not take her eyes from her baby, but moved her lips slowly in response, "If there is," she said, pressing Hitty's tiny hand to her cheek, "he is no friend of the weak."

Sabrina and Joseph
(1690)

irty, floppy ears bobbed enthusiastically as scrunched snouts sniffed out and inhaled the browned cabbage leaves, eggshells, and various vegetable shavings that had been dropped on the muddy ground. Sabrina set the rope handle of her wooden bucket down and wiped both her hands in one long motion down the front of her apron. The air was cool and wet, of the nature that would capture the vapors of her breath in a visible curling puff for only a moment. Sabrina surveyed the countryside where she stood, taking in the creeping fog. It ran down from the hillside as if it knew its hour had come, for as the rising sun advanced, its reign over the grasslands drew to a close. She released a final exhale, letting out another long curl of white breath, and then picked up her bucket, turning away from the exuberant feasters to walk back up the hill toward her home.

Sabrina quickened her pace at the sight of smoke rising from their stone chimney, eager to warm her chilled fingers against the pulse of the fire. She pushed into the front door in a hurry and flung her empty bucket down, breathless from the march up the wet grassy incline.

"Ah, Sabrina!" Sabrina's mother sat at their primitive wooden table in the center of their cottage, her hands folded on it respectfully. The outline of a darker and larger figure stood next to the freshly built fire, seemingly being warmed in the same way Sabrina had hoped to be. "You do recall Master Joseph, don't you Sabrina? And the pleasure we had of meeting him not more than three years ago?"

Her mother swiveled in her seat abruptly to smile toward the man who stood casually behind her. "How it possibly could have been three years, I confess . . ." her voice trailed off and she cleared her throat, straightening her stature and returning her gaze toward Sabrina.

"Come sit down, Sabrina." Sabrina did not move from the door, her eyes fixed toward Joseph's outline.

"Mother," Sabrina's response was stiff. "The pigs have been fed. I am going out now in search of more firewood," she said, opening the door. "We must keep our swine both fat and warm, mustn't we?" And with a look of contempt cast toward the shadowy figure, she stomped across the threshold.

The sound of her mother's protest barely reached Sabrina's ears before it was snapped off by the slam of the door behind her. Sabrina advanced toward the tree line that sat behind the cottage she and her mother shared. Her eyes narrowed, and her nostrils flared. The second opening and closing of the cottage door behind Sabrina announced the pursuit of Master Joseph who had just emerged, his brow furrowed in an uncomfortable way.

"Sabrina!" he called after her, "please, if I may have a word."

Sabrina ignored his voice, continuing her march toward the forest. "It is about your sister!" he persisted, quickening his pace.

Sabrina paused, refusing to turn to face the man but unable to continue to ignore him.

Joseph arrived at her side, fairly out of breath and visibly flustered. "What of her?" Sabrina asked, her words sharp with disdain for the one she addressed.

"She . . ." Jospeh took another great inhale, still unrecovered from his efforts to pursue Sabrina. "She is unwell."

Sabrina's countenance softened into one of worry, and she finally turned to face Joseph.

"How do you mean?" she inquired, now intently studying the face she had so purposefully avoided gazing upon up until this point.

"She . . ." Joseph shifted his body weight and looked away, seemingly unsure of how to continue. "She was with child," he said. His eyebrows furrowed again with discomfort, more from the awkwardness of his own words than from the pain they were about to inflict.

Sabrina's eyes and mouth widened, unsure of what to feel.

"Oh," she said, unsure at first. "Oh!" she exclaimed, now beginning to grow in excitement. "How has she fared? Is the child healthy? You said 'was.' Has she given birth already?" Joseph shifted his gaze down toward his boots and kicked at a loose rock.

"The child has been born," he said. Sabrina's face brightened at the joyful news, then fell as she watched a reticent look cover Joseph's face.

"And Mary?" Sabrina asked. "How is my sister?" Jospeh said nothing, his fixation with the rock growing in intensity. "Joseph!" Sabrina snapped, desperation taking over her body.

"She is . . ." Joseph shook his head, and then stared up at the sky awkwardly before closing his eyes tightly. "She is . . . not. And I . . . ," he shook his head, "I cannot take the child."

Sabrina stared at him in disbelief, anguish, and disgust, her eyes full of questions, "What could you possibly mean," her eyes now filling with angry tears, "you cannot take the child?"

"It would not suit. My mother would never allow the child of another woman to . . . how would that reflect upon me? I am . . ." Joseph stumbled around with his words before pausing and placing his hands over his eyes. "I am to marry a woman of good status. It was arranged by my mother and father, and it is to be of good fortune not just for me but for the reputation of my whole family. It is to be a good match, truthfully, not a mistake like . . ." Joseph's voice trailed off and he stood in silence for a moment. His countenance was grave.

Sabrina stared past him as if he had vanished altogether, her mouth now dry and somehow empty of the words that had, just a few moments ago, been ready to leap from her tongue and strangle the man who stood before her. Finally, Sabrina inhaled deeply and asked, with eyes still averted, "How long has my sister been dead?"

Without looking up, Joseph mumbled, "Two weeks."

Sabrina sat down in the dry grass and covered her head with her hands.

"I'll bring the child to you tomorrow. Her name is Alice." And without another word, Joseph turned and walked away.

Joseph and Henry
(1660)

A small bird hopped curiously upon the dewy grass, searching intently, it seemed, for some secret or perhaps meal that lay within its tresses. Joseph sat as still as he could, barely allowing breath to pass through his small lips lest he frighten the feathered huntress away. The snap of a dry stick startled both the boy and the bird, breaking the moment of wonder. Joseph turned to see his father Henry standing over him, his countenance vacant as usual. He fondled the frills of his cuff with one hand and with the other, straightened a brass button on his vest. Joseph did not feel much when he looked at his father, except perhaps a small twinge of disappointment. The time that was shared by the pair of them was not particularly amusing to Joseph, and he often found himself looking for ways to break away as soon as possible whenever they were together.

Henry's ears perked up at the sound of his three older sisters' gleeful laughter floating over the garden shrubbery that hid their play from his sight. Cosette, Fiona, and Marguerite had all been born into the line of Du Hamel prior to Joseph's arrival. In their own right, the girls were rays of light, with infinitely delightful dispositions. There was never a shortage of vivacity when a space was allowed for its expression, a luxury not afforded at all to Joseph as he had been, of the four children, the one ultimately hoped for. He was therefore kept close to his father's side and, more importantly, held to a higher standard of behavior. The favor bequeathed to Joseph was indeed, to him, a heavy and unwanted burden.

"Join me for a stroll in the gardens, Joseph," Henry said, pressing the back of his hand into the palm of the other behind him.

Joseph came to his feet, vexed that his moment of stillness with the birds had been interrupted. The sweet aroma of damp petals and black earth filled Joseph's nose as he followed his father's prettily painted coat and neat, white curls.

"Do you," began his father who at that moment was studying a small beetle climbing over the leaf of a boxwood, "understand the time and attention that such a fantastic garden demands in order for its beauty to be maintained?" he asked, flicking the beetle away.

Joseph nodded lazily, infinitely bored by the direction the conversation was taking.

"It is immense," his father said, turning to fix widened eyes on his son, his brows raised emphatically. Turning again, Henry resumed his strolling and lecture, "The time! The time it took to not only put these roots in the ground, but for them to grow to become as glorious as they are," he exclaimed, motioning to the height of a nearby topiary, "is something that should not be taken for granted or," and upon this word he whirled again to face Joseph, this time with a wagging finger, "wasted!"

Joseph continued to nod, familiar with the words his father was once again imparting to him.

Henry's recitation was interrupted the next moment, however, when the sound of breaking brush and a shriek of laughter landed Henry's youngest sister, Marguerite, upon the path ahead of them. She had tumbled through a plot of shrubbery made up primarily of lavender and rosemary, likely after having fled from the pursuit of her older sisters in a game of chase. Marguerite now sat, legs splayed, face red from the heat of running and laughing, and eyes bright with delight. A wake of crushed and bruised bushes marked the path she had taken.

Joseph's spontaneous reaction of a laugh was swallowed immediately in response to his father's booming voice. "No!" he shouted, crossing the space between himself and Marguerite in two giant strides. His face was red, and veins bulged in his neck and forehead as he reached down and grabbed a clump of Marguerite's golden ringlets and ripped her up off the ground.

"You stupid, selfish, child!" he yelled, holding her face so close to his own that his breath made her eyes flinch. "Your frivolous, foolish play has crushed a living thing! Keep your witless self out of the garden, or damn it, I'll crush you!"

And with those words, he flung his daughter down, sending her skidding across the pebble path with a spray of small rocks flying up around her. Marguerite's eyes were wide with terror; her arms and legs trembled uncontrollably. She sat for a moment, a petrified animal, uncertain whether it would be safer to remain motionless or flee. Then, in the same moment that her tears began to flood her eyes, Marguerite scrambled to her feet and ran, her tattered dress dropping rocks, and small twigs of lavender and rosemary that had gotten caught up in its fabric.

Henry straightened, flexing the fingers of his hand that had just been grasping the strands of his daughter's silken blonde hair. "So, you see," he exhaled, seeming to compose himself, "you can't just let any idiot into your garden. You must take great care to preserve it."

Henry and Adam
(1610)

Henry's blonde ringlets streamed behind him as he ran shrieking with glee across the pebble-strewn seashore. A posse of gulls would collect on the verge, eyeing him suspiciously. He, in turn, would pause his wilding and return their stares with a playful ember of mischief flickering in his eyes before suddenly breaking the tension with a squawk of gladness and charging into the center of the amassed spindly sea birds. The gulls would scatter in agitation before reuniting again on the opposite end of the shore, anticipating the next onslaught of childish exuberance.

The volley of disruption, dispersion, and communion would likely have gone on for hours. The sun hung unhurried just above the sea line, not yet painting with any red or purple shades, only casting a golden hue over every surface upon which it fell. Henry rarely tired from such play, but he was suddenly distracted by the scurrying of a small creature among the larger, drier rocks farther up the shore. Not one to give up the opportunity to meet another playmate, Henry departed from his game with the gulls and began clambering over the rugged terrain to reach the one that scuttled. He found, to his joy, a large hermit crab sitting comfortably in the sand between two wedged rocks, a trail of delicate dots and lines left in the wake of his path. The sound of more tiny claws on rocks and an awful scent caused Henry to lift his gaze again and look farther up the shore where the base of the overhanging cliff met the sand. A small gathering of hermit crabs was migrating to and from a small mound shrouded by a dirtied cloth.

Persistent curiosity brought Henry's feet closer to the colony until something inside his small body stopped him. He dared not tread one step closer. An unfamiliar fear poured over Henry, and the light within his small eyes vanished. Panic rose in his heart as he realized he was frozen in place, unable to move from his unexplained terror.

"Poppa!" Henry called, rooted in place. "Poppa, come!"

Henry's father who had, up until that point, been strolling the beach with Henry's mother, heard his son and came to Henry's side.

"Henry," he said, looking expectantly at him, "for what reason have I been disrupted from my leisure?"

Henry's mother arrived as his father spoke these words, and looking past her son, let out a gasp and put a hand to her mouth. An expression of shock and horror fell upon her face like a shadow, and the gravity that Henry had sensed in the air of this corner of the seaside was confirmed by the death being reflected to him in his mother's eyes.

Henry's father, Adam, followed her gaze to the small mound of cloth covered in hermit crabs. His lips hardened into a flat, pressed line, and his expression became stony. "Son," Adam said sharply, "come away from this place."

But Henry could not move, still not understanding what it was that he was being both drawn toward and repulsed by. This foul-smelling bundle held an immense weight. His young, honest mind had not yet learned to tune out the voices of the rest of his being, and so he stood, listening to the whispers of profound grief that his innocent heart could not comprehend.

"Poppa," Henry asked again, "what is it?"

Henry's father straightened and lifted his chin, his gaze now looking upward toward the ledge of the cliff that hung above them. "Unwanted refuse," Adam said flatly, his eyes still hard and cold.

"Adam!" Henry's mother's eyes turned incredulous as she looked at her husband with a new expression of horror.

"Come away, Henry!" Adam's voice had changed to anger. "There is no sense in lingering here."

Henry's mother lightly touched Adam's arm and, with reticence, whispered, "Ought we not bury it?"

Adam looked at his wife with disgust, but his countenance softened by just the smallest fraction. With a jerk, Adam pulled his arm away from his wife and strode angrily toward the bundle. Grabbing a nearby piece of driftwood, Adam flicked the clambering hermits from the bundle and lifted a corner of the fabric. A pungent smell burst forth immediately, and the three of them put their hands to their mouths and noses in unison.

Adam stood looking for no more than an instant before he flung the stick away and began to march back toward shore, grabbing Henry roughly by the arm on his way. Henry's mother lingered for a moment, seemingly experiencing the same pull to stay by the abandoned bundle that Henry had felt.

"Dear!" she called after a pause, "will you not . . ." her words were cut off by Adam who, without glancing back, shouted, "It's a girl!"

Adam and Lada
(1570)

The sound of shrieking filled the muddy streets of Novgorod. Hundreds of men and women streamed past Adam's dirty, frosted windowpane, fleeing from a terror that could not yet be seen. A burst of flame in a neighboring home across the thoroughfare invoked heightened panic, and a burst of frantic men and women came crashing through the threshold of Adam's home, seeking immediate shelter from the devil on their heels. Adam's voice joined in with the cries of terror and confusion as he backed into the farthest corner of his family's humble izba, finding refuge beneath a cot in the back of the hut. A large-bellied man with a beard full of vomit and a wild look in his eyes tripped inside the door and landed heavily atop a frail-looking woman who had been among the first to erupt into the home. They collapsed—he on top of her small form, and she began to scream even louder, trying with all her might to wriggle out from under his ponderous body.

"Get off me!" she yelled, kicking at his belly with her pinned knees. The man began to scramble upward, pushing with his stout arms to right himself. But no sooner had he got his hands pressed firmly to the floor, than two men dressed from head to toe in black—eyes full of darkness and bloodthirst—pushed through the door, bringing a sword swiftly down into the back of the weighty, bearded man. Adam watched as the clumsy, great man's face froze in an expression of agony, his eyes growing dim before extinguishing altogether. From his parted pale lips, still fixed wide-open, a small stream of blood and saliva dripped onto the face of the panicked woman who lay trapped beneath his deadweight.

Adam held his breath and kept quiet, watching from beneath the cot as the two evil men devoured with their swords each man, woman, and child who had sought sanctuary in his home. The woman pinned beneath the dead man's body, whether unnoticed or left intentionally by the bloodthirsty raiders, remained alive. As soon as the two men departed with their swords, she began to fight with all her might to free her body from the deadweight that suppressed her, but all her effort was in vain. Adam remained in his corner until another burst of light and the sound of glass shattering set the tumbledown izba aflame.

Adam scrambled out from his hiding place, his heart about to burst from his chest. The blaze took to the dry wood and straw-stuffed furnishings as if it had been prepared for the very purpose of being burned. Suffocating heat and the deafening crackle of his home being consumed overwhelmed Adam as he sought to escape from his ignited shelter.

"Wait!" the scream of the small woman trapped beneath the weight of a dead man interrupted Adam's flight for only a moment. He looked at her—her eyes wide with terror and fear. "Please!" she begged, her voice throbbing with desperation. "Help me! Help me, please! Do not leave me. My name is Lada. I am a mother. I have children. Please, please help me go to them!"

Adam stood with his feet rooted in place, unable to walk away from this helpless creature. Taking several steps back, Adam grabbed ahold of the large man's arm and gave a mighty heave. The man did not move an inch.

"Again!" screamed Lada. "I'll push too!"

So again, Adam and Lada fought to remove his hefty form, and again, they failed. A thunderous crash brought an overhead beam down upon the cot beneath which Adam had just been hiding, crushing it entirely and setting fire to the whole back corner of the small room. Adam was startled, and he moved away from Lada, again pursuing freedom from the impending flames.

"Don't leave me here!" Lada screamed, her voice somehow holding both the fear that comes from the realization that death has arrived as well as the conviction of one who still has hope. Adam turned back one last time, looking into Lada's frightened eyes, streaming heavily with tears. Staring back with panic and fear, Adam held both of his hands up in surrender.

"I . . . I am sorry," he offered. And turning, he fled from the burning home to escape into the frozen, blood-stained streets.

Lada and Kaleb
(1540)

L ada blew fervently on her left fingertips, imparting to her best ability a burst of warmth onto her chilled, white extremities. She sat in the corner of her family's small hut, moving a steel comb rhythmically through the fibers of a thick clump of wool. A soft freshly carded pile had grown steadily from early that morning when Lada had first sat down to the task of preparing her textiles for weaving. A small whimper from a crude pallet of blankets folded on the floor caused Lada to put down her work for a moment.

"Shush, shush, my darling," cooed Lada, softly stroking the top of her infant's head. "I won't be much longer, my dear Ana, and then we will go out into the world."

The touch of her mother calmed the unsettled baby, and she returned to her peaceful doze for a moment more. Lada fetched a large basket from against the wall and began to stuff her morning's work into it. Shouldering the straps of the overflowing hamper, Lada wrapped her daughter heavily in more roughly woven blankets and furs before tying her tightly to her chest. Ana protested from the jostle for only a moment before settling back down contentedly to the sound of her mother's heartbeat and breath. A glacial burst of air exhaled into Lada's face as she pushed open the primitive wooden door of their shanty. Snow and ice laid thickly on the streets, doing its best to cover the tracks of boots, carts, hooves, and feces that somehow still managed to remain, no matter how heavily it snowed. This was not unusual for springtime in Russia as the cold never seemed to depart in haste. However, there was a lightness in Lada's step as she took to the frozen streets.

It was payday. The work of caring for her sheep all year, sheering them in the spring, and carding their wool, was a process that demanded all Lada's energy and patience. To finally see the benefits of her toil was not just something she looked forward to, it was how she and her children survived. Lada picked her way along the road, steering clear of carts that may drop their great wooden wheels into muddy holes and send a spray of frozen water over her and her precious cargo.

Her business was with a man with whom she had worked for over five years. He was a gentle and kind spirit who wove her precious wool into thick blankets and heavy coats. Indeed, some of the blankets with which her daughter was now wrapped had been made by her friend Anatoli's hands.

This meeting, a time in which she handed off her carefully carded wool to be made into something of beauty, was as seasonally expected as the chill that remained during spring-time. Upon her arrival at the door of Anatoli's home and shop, Lada knocked her makeshift boots off carefully on the rough wooden post of the awning before stepping gingerly over the threshold.

"Anatoli!" she called joyfully, "I come bearing gifts!" A scraping sound from the back room and a seemingly agitated grunt of effort suggested that a great man was rising from a wooden chair that sat close to the floor. A moment later, a man did indeed appear before Lada, though he was not great in size. On the contrary, he was quite small in stature, and his frame was of the kind that had been built solely from being well-fed and never lifting a finger. His face was clean-shaven, and his eyes were sharp, black, and quick, like little gnats. He had a nose of equal sharpness with nostrils that flared widely when he spoke and a mouth as hard and flat as a charcoal stick.

"What business do you have with Anatoli?" he asked boredly, clearly annoyed that he had been interrupted from his sitting. Unphased by the small man's rudeness, Lada shifted her brimming basket stuffed with wool from her shoulders and placed it expectantly before him. Her daughter squirmed momentarily, slightly aroused by the change in position, before settling down again, always content to be close to her mother's chest.

"I brought my freshly carded wool to sell to him for his

textiles," she said, her eyes possessing a small glint of pride in her work. The man looked down at the basket for a moment before picking it up and buoying it lightly up and down in his hands.

"Anatoli is gone," he said dully, his eyes staring blankly toward the back stone wall. "My name is Kaleb, and this is now my shop."

Lada looked around, confused by this unexpected news. The shop looked just as it always had. Large stacks of blankets, looms, and drying threads hung about the room, and baskets of fully threaded bobbins sat mounded on roughly hewn shelves. Not a hint of change apart from the distinct disparity between the two men was to be seen.

"I see," said Lada, trying her best to hide her disappointment. "Well," she continued lightly, looking at Kaleb with expectation, "I am happy to do business with you nonetheless!"

Kaleb did not respond but took the basket to the back room from which he had first appeared and returned carrying a small leather pouch. From it he tipped a handful of coins, which he counted out carefully before returning a few to the pouch. Pocketing it again, he dropped the coppers into Lada's open palm before turning away to rejoin with his squatty wooden chair. Lada needed only to feel the weight of the coins in her hand to know that it was not nearly enough.

"Kaleb," she said hesitantly, "forgive me, but this is not even a quarter of what I am owed."

Kaleb turned to her slowly, and with the same bored expression on his face replied, "It is my price for what you have brought. Take it or leave it."

Lada stood, fingering the small fistful of coins, trying to calm her heartbeat. It would not be near enough to provide what little she and her family survived on. Indeed, they barely made it by as it was, and this amount was, as she said, less than a quarter of that meager livelihood.

"I cannot take it," she said, unsure of what else to do. There were no other weavers in her province that she knew of, but she was certain she could not part with her wool for so little. Perhaps she could travel to the next town and try to find a fair price?

Kaleb returned to his back room in exasperation, and after another moment returned with her basket. He plopped it down in front of her and stuck out his hand for his coins. Lada dropped them obligingly into his pudgy fist and was about to reshoulder her wares until she looked inside. An enormous mound of her wool had been scooped from the top, and the lesser part of half her wool remained. Lada's mouth hung open for a moment before she looked up to meet the expectant and glowering eyes of Kaleb.

"You have taken half my wool!" she exclaimed, fighting back tears of panic. Lada saw the faintest hint of a smile edge around the corner of Kaleb's pale, thin lips before he again turned to retreat to the back room.

"Wait," Lada said, grabbing him by the arm in protest of his departure, but he spun around immediately and shoved her back, sending her and her daughter tumbling into her half empty basket, knocking the remaining wool onto the dirty, straw strewn floor. Ana broke out into a loud wail of surprise from the sudden fall, and the tears finally broke forth in Lada's eyes.

"Take your screaming brat and get out of my shop," Kaleb said hotly, "I didn't take anything from you." And with a look made stupid with contempt, turned on his heels to leave Lada to collect what was left of her livelihood.

Kaleb and Jurar
(1500)

The thunder did not come from the sky, but rumbled up from the hard, packed earth. Kaleb was familiar with this sensation of the ground rattling beneath his feet. It was the same as a knock on the door or the ringing of a bell that announced the return of the horsemen. Kaleb pattered to the pine shelters that stood across the plain from his village, waiting to receive the approaching band of horses. Water and feed for the beasts would be the first priority upon the arrival of the returning nomads. Their lives depended on these creatures, and they were cared for accordingly. A well stood off about fifty paces from where the animals' stables had been erected for the duration of the Kazakh's time in this region.

Kaleb had been assigned the task of drawing and carrying the glacial water from the source and bringing it to the thirsty steeds upon their arrival. The work was not easy, but Kaleb's love of the horses gave meaning to his effort. He heaved and pulled with all his weight to bring one bucket to the top of the borehole, and almost inevitably soaked the front of his fur ton and trousers as he dragged it to the stables. His bare, small hands turned red from the biting air that whipped over them, freezing the water that would splash periodically as he carried his bucket back and forth to the water troughs. He worked until every basin was full, waiting for the hot, thirsty muzzles of the men's horses to dip into. The growl of the thundering hooves grew deeper and louder as the band approached.

Kaleb stood expectantly as the mass of man and beast grew slowly from a small line in the distance to a wave of a powerful force descending on the valley. Kaleb faced the direction from which the mighty sea of warriors approached, feeling the tremors of many pounding hooves move through his whole body like a current. A feeling of deep desire surged up inside Kaleb's young chest—a desire for that same kind of power, a force to be wielded and reckoned with. It would only be a few moments more before the horses arrived, and Kaleb would be able to feel the waves of their exerted energy roll off them, like a tide. His favorite thing was to stand at the side of a horse that had just galloped for many miles and bask in the heat of its heaving flank as it washed over him. He ate it up like a starving child would devour a hot cake and longed for those sparse moments in which he could vicariously live through the radiant energy of a body emanating power.

"Kaleb!" the voice of Turar, his elder brother by twelve years, sliced through his meditation about hooves. "Bring another bucket of water back from the well!" he called.

Kaleb stood still and unresponsive, unwilling to give up the precious approaching time he sought to share with the descending band of horses.

"Kaleb!" he shouted again, "I know you aren't deaf! You're worthless elsewise. Bring the water and stop ignoring me!"

Kaleb did not flinch at his brother's biting words but stood rigidly, refusing to even look in the direction from which Turar's voice traveled. The sound of the soft thud of a young man's feet joined in with the vibrations of the approaching steeds, and Kaleb knew his brother was seeking vengeance for his baby brother's ignorance.

"Idiot!" Turar shouted, "for someone who has so little to contribute, I'd think you'd at least make yourself useful in the little that is asked of you!" Kaleb braced himself for a box on the ears, but a hand never fell.

He felt Turar standing over him, a different kind of energy pouring over him than what he experienced next to the horses. The heat that radiated from his brother did not fill Kaleb with a sense of longing or of vicariously lived power; it made him feel small, vulnerable, and frightened. But Kaleb remained where he was, unwilling to shrink away from his older brother's towering presence. He felt Turar's cold hand grasp his own small, red ones and drop the handle of the bucket into them.

"Fetch the water, little one," Turar said scornfully, daring his young brother with his words to challenge him. Kaleb grasped the bucket, and without a word, turned toward the direction he instinctively knew the well to be in. He moved to take one step and immediately toppled over Turar's extended leg, falling face first onto the frozen, cracked earth. The hollow thud of the bucket landing sounded some distance off in the plain and the guffaw of Turar immediately rang in the air, somehow drowning out the thunderous din of the arrival of many horses.

Kaleb felt Turar lean over him and spit mockingly in his ear, "Your eyes aren't the only blind thing about you. You clearly can't see that this is your place. Here, in the dirt. Remember that next time you get too proud to fetch your mother water. Now go find your bucket, silly boy."

Turar and Aliner
(1488)

The embers of the night's fire were just beginning to die down. The last flame had withered more than ten minutes before, and now the coals sat, fading in their glow, but still somehow emitting the precious warmth that kept Turar squatting quietly and motionlessly before them. It was not just the heat of the dying fire that kept Turar here, outside by this ring of stones and ash. The desire to remain outdoors, in the open and away from his family's tent, was another, and perhaps the most prominent motivation for Turar to stay where he was, wishing the sun had never set. The movement of a heavy tapestry and the croaking sound of his grandfather's voice broke the enchantment of the orange glow.

"Turar, night has fallen," Aliner said, his voice as dusty and graven as the pit Turar now bent over.

"Yes, Aliner," Turar replied, rising from his warming perch as slowly as he was able. The vastness of the sky was apparent from the clearness of the air and brightness of the stars that night. They shimmered and glinted like the silver reflections of the sunlight on water, giving off a glow of their own that did not look like it would ever fade. The warmth and glow that had rested on Turar's small, red face as he sat gazing at the fire, however, had already gone out. His face was now cold, as it turned toward his grandfather who stood towering at the tent's entrance.

As he looked at the old man, frail in stature but somehow still domineering and frightening, that chill traveled from his cheeks and into his very core. Aliner stood to the side just enough to allow Turar to pass through the entrance of the family tent. His mother dozed quietly in the corner, undisturbed by the sound of movement or the rush of chilled air that had come from the opening of the tent's entrance. Turar's father was away, and his grandmother had passed. He was, in essence, alone with his grandfather.

"Remove your shoes, Turar," Aliner rasped, his voice just as weak yet somehow just as frightening as the old man's appearance.

Turar obeyed, slipping off the colorful moccasins he wore every day.

"Wash your hands, Turar," Aliner said, his words labored but still full of power. Turar obeyed, scooping a handful of the cold water that sat in a basin on the packed earthen floor of their tent, and rubbed it carefully between his tiny fingers.

"Wash your face, Turar." Turar did. "Now, help your ata, Turar." Turar was familiar with what Aliner's expectations were after he spoke these words. The familiar dread landed at the base of Turar's stomach like a small stone in a river as slowly he began to remove his grandfather's head dress, then robe, shirt, and britches. Taking the small basin of water from the ground and a rough cloth from a folded stack that sat next to it, Turar began to systemically wash his grandfather's naked body.

"The water is cold, Turar. I need your warm breath on my skin." Obediently, Turar would wipe away the dirt and sweat on his grandfather's sagging, thin skin, and then breathe hotly over the place he had just cleaned, giving his all to please his ata. He worked diligently, starting with his wrinkled face and working his way down his bony arms and sunken chest.

"Slow down, Turar," his grandfather whispered, as Turar hurried past Aliner's groin with the cloth. "Do not neglect me."

Turar, again obeyed, moving the damp rag back up his grandfather's thin legs to wash and breathe on his inner thighs and genitals. A deep exhale from Aliner caused Turar to look up at his grandfather's face. Aliner's eyes were closed, and his face was contorted in an expression that made Turar's stomach turn sour. As quickly as he felt he could without angering his grandfather, Turar finished bathing his ata, then helped him into his clean clothes.

"Sleep now, Turar," Aliner said, gravely, moving away to lie down on his own mat. Turar laid down, but he could not obey this final command.

Aliner and Saray
(1401)

Aliner pattered down the streets of Damascus, clutching the hem of his mother's thob while doing his part to keep pace with her hurried footsteps. Broken pottery, muddy holes, and general animal waste littered the packed earthen path.

"Hurry, now," his mother, Saray, urged. "We seek refuge."

Aliner was unsure whether his mother was speaking to her five children who straggled along beside her or to herself, but he listened and picked up his tiny feet, working hard to maintain a speed that matched his mother's quiet but apparent fear. The dwindling light of the setting sun was shortening the length of its remaining rays, pulling back its extended arms to bid the city goodnight. The day had held much turmoil that Aliner had not understood. A sudden ransacking of Damascus had begun before the dawn of that day, with cries for mercy, the crackle of erupting flames, and the clatter of homes being pillaged ringing out from every direction.

Aliner's father, Hassan, had burst into their home, calling his family to himself. "We must take refuge!" he cried between deep inhales, his eyes wild with horror, sweat still dripping from his red brow as he struggled to regain his breath. "Allah has provided refuge!"

Aliner's mother, Saray, had grasped Hassan's hand. "It is God's will! Where are we to go?" Hassan took their youngest, the infant Nour, from Saray's other arm and flung open the door. "We've been promised safety if we can make it to the Mosque!" he said, ushering Aliner and the other children out the door. "Hurry!" he urged, "they are coming!"

The family stole through the streets, keeping to the quietest alleys and the darkest corners. All around them, Aliner heard screams of terror and the shattering of glass. Aliner kept his eyes downcast and averted from the sights that his ears told him were all about him, but his heart still raced as he kept to his mother's side, obedient to follow where they were being led. The enormous painted dome of the mosque loomed in the distance, but as they drew closer to the immense structure, an inexplicable panic burst into Aliner's chest, that was somehow new despite the destruction that had been taking place all about him since daybreak. Families that Aliner recognized as belonging to the fellow priests of the Umayyad streamed into the open door of the waiting Mosque like water into a gaping mouth. A final street stretched between Aliner and his family and the entrance of the place where they had been promised safety.

"Come!" his father called, as he made a final push across the street while clutching Nour with one arm and pulling his older sister with the other. His mother looked down at him and his other brother and sister and whispered, "Stay by me!" Then clutching his brother's and sister's arms, she rushed toward the open door. Aliner picked up his feet, trying to obey his mother's command, but no sooner had he advanced into the frantic street than he was knocked to the ground by a stampede of fleeing men and women. Aliner crawled from the center of the chaos back into the shadows of the darkened alley from which he and his family had just emerged. Saray stood on the steps of the mosque with tears streaming from her eyes, crying out his name, unable to see her son from where she stood. Aliner heard his father say, "Saray! Come! He is lost!"

And with great effort, he pulled his wife back into the opening of the building. Aliner scrambled to his feet, trying to muster his courage to advance back into the fray. He was about to make another effort to cross the river of citizens when he saw several men, clad in armor, shut the door of the mosque and bar it with an enormous beam. Torches were brought and, within the next moment, the mosque was set ablaze. The panic in the city rose to new heights as this symbol of fortitude and purpose was irreverently dismantled. The voices of those trapped inside joined with the screams of the rest of those who were being destroyed within the city, and Aliner, still hiding inside the dark shadows of the alley, watched as his family perished.

Saray and Aisha
(1376)

"Be good and do not make a sound," Saray heard as she laid on her back in her family's small home fighting back the urge to vomit. The floor was cool to the touch and in a strange way, it helped to calm her nerves.

Today was the day that Saray had anticipated for many years, never expecting that she would be able to avoid it. Nevertheless, her body told her that what was about to happen to her was not natural or good. Saray's mother, Aisha, and a local midwife kneeled at Saray's feet. Aisha had hired the best woman for the job and Saray was told to trust her. She was skilled, meticulous, and knew how to cut and pack the incisions to ensure that infection would be very unlikely. This was custom for every woman, so why was Saray's body shaking so uncontrollably? Why did she have to fight the urge to kick her mother and the midwife in their faces and run? Aisha wiped a strand of damp hair from her daughter's sweaty forehead and gave her a knowing smile.

"You are strong, Saray," she said encouragingly, "becoming a real woman."

Saray did her best to smile back and shine bravery from her face, but her expression immediately contorted into one of agony as the renowned midwife brought the razor blade between Saray's opened thighs. For a moment, Saray thought she was indeed going to vomit. Aisha, sensing this, offered an empty bowl and a hand to lift her head, but the sensation passed, and Saray relaxed her chest and neck back down, suddenly feeling quite lightheaded. The midwife bound Saray's legs together at the upper thigh and knee and gave Aisha instructions on how to care for her daughter during the healing period.

"Do not untie the bandages or let her stand or walk for several days. If she must relieve herself, then you are responsible for lifting her up and cleaning her well to prevent infection."

"We are eternally grateful for you and your work," Aisha said as she walked the midwife to the door. "You serve the women of our city well."

Praise for an act, that to Saray felt more like violence than a gift, departing from the lips of her mother caused a different kind of wound to open in Saray's chest. It felt like betrayal. Saray, with legs bound, rolled over onto her side to face the wall, keeping her back to the two women who stood chatting in the open door. They spoke lightly, as if the three of them had just shared an afternoon tea. A rift had been created between, not only Saray and her mother, but Saray and herself that she did not understand.

Aisha told her that she was now a woman. So why did she feel as though she had just lost something? Softly and quietly, so as not to disobey her mother, Saray lay on the cool floor of their family's home and wept.

Aisha and Ra`ah
(1340)

The air was full of salt and light and the scent of spices. The sound of creaking boards and tensioned ropes bobbed through the air like the ships that rocked in the port as large imports from faraway lands were unloaded from within their hulls. Aisha stood a few paces from one such ship, her eyes fixed on the men moving the cargo. She clutched a colorful satchel to her chest with both hands, shyly searching behind each dark beard for a pair of kind eyes.

She found them in the face of an older sailor whose beard had already turned white and whose face possessed the soft brushstrokes of time. Aisha inhaled deeply, pulling together her courage to emerge from her safe perch of observation and approach him. He paused as she came forward and smiled kindly, placing his hand on the top of a pottery vessel that had just been unloaded.

"Good morning," Aisha said quietly with a smile. "I am here to buy your sugar."

The old man smiled widely, revealing bare pink gums and a radiant light in his eyes. "We will be happy to sell you our sugar, little one," he replied, "but we have just begun to unload our goods. The market is where you can buy your sugar."

Aisha looked down at her small colorful purse, somewhat embarrassed. "I know, but . . ." Aisha blushed, "I have a difficult time getting any at the market before it is gone."

The old man's face reflected understanding. The market was not always an easy place to navigate, and sugar was a treat that was in high demand. He pressed a finger to his lips and tapped the lid of the ceramic jar he stood next to. "For you, this once," he whispered.

Aisha's face lit up as she watched the old man scoop the tiny crystals into a sack. She emptied her pouch into the open, weathered palm of the old man, and he handed her the sugar, smiling widely. "Thank you!" she exclaimed, before spinning on her heels and taking off in a sprint toward her home.

When she arrived, Aisha threw her shawl and empty coin pouch to the side and brought her sugar to the rough wooden table that stood in the corner of her family's home. Bowls sat patiently, already filled with the ingredients that Aisha anticipated needing. She set to work, mixing her spices, flour, eggs, and the precious sugar she had labored to obtain. After stoking the fire, Aisha formed her mixture into a small cake and placed it carefully among the coals. She sat by it patiently, watching as it bubbled, browned, and rose. She took a small stick and poked the top of it tenderly once she suspected it was done, just as she had watched her mother do. A clean tip confirmed her suspicions, and she gingerly pulled a cake from the embers, brushing away the glowing specks that clung to the earthen dish. Aisha smiled softly to herself as she admired her hard work, exhaling with satisfaction at her labor of love brought to completion.

The sun had been setting slowly while Aisha baked. She sat holding her small sugar cake, waiting for her father to return home in his boat after his long hours of fishing. The dark crept in, and the night grew deeper as Aisha sat quietly just inside the stoop of her home. Hours passed, and Aisha's head slowly drooped and nodded before she shook herself awake again, determined to stay awake for her father.

The sun was only just beginning to rise with the slightest blossoms of rose leaching into the sky before the sound of the front door moving on its old hinges finally brought Aisha to full attention. She jumped to her feet, cradling her cold cake just as her father, Ra`ah walked through the threshold. His eyes were tired, and his shoulders slumped in defeat and exhaustion. "Welcome home, Ab!" Aisha said quietly, "Did you catch many fish?"

Ra`ah lifted his gaze from the floor to meet the eyes of his adoring daughter. Smiling weakly, he replied, "No, my love. I did not catch any."

Aisha felt the weight that she knew her father felt sink

into her own stomach. "That is alright, Ab," Aisha replied lightly, attempting to lift her father's spirits. "I know that tomorrow, you will catch even more fish than you usually do!"

Ra`ah attempted to smile, but the heaviness of his worry seemed to weigh down his countenance.

"Here, Ab!" Aisha said, attempting to shift her father's thoughts from his despair. She pressed her cold sugar cake into his palm proudly, then embraced him. "This is to celebrate the day you were born!"

Ra`ah looked down at the cake for a moment before a dark cloud came over his eyes. "Aisha," he said, his voice still calm but somehow harder, "how much did you spend to make this cake?"

Aisha stood for a moment, caught off guard by her father's response to her gesture of love. "I . . ." Aisha looked at the cake and then back up to her Ab. "It is alright, Ab. I used all my own coins."

Ra`ah's eyes remained heavy. Slowly he placed the cake down on the table and rubbed his hands over his face. "This was a foolish thing to do, Aisha," he said, "we might have needed your coins for basic food to survive. We cannot afford something as extravagant as sugar and spices."

Ra`ah looked again at the cake with disdain then back again at Aisha's face and said, "You will eat this cake. I will not have you go hungry. But remember with every bite, that it is because of you and your foolish decision that I must go hungry."

Aisha stood, fighting back tears as she listened to her father's words of reproach. "I love you, Ab," Aisha said finally, trying to pick up the pieces of her shattered gift.

"I love you too, daughter," Ra`ah replied.

Ra`ah and Aziza
(1290)

A loud slap rang through the air, juxtaposed by the eerily calm voice of a woman. "Do not be foolish!" the voice commanded as another smack cracked the stillness.

Ra`ah stood backed into the corner of a stone wall in the courtyard of his family's home, his face, arms, legs, and bare chest streaked with the red welts left by the wooden shoot that his mother stood white knuckling in her fist.

"Just confess to me what we both know to be true," she insisted, doing her best to reel her power over her son back in.

"Mama, please!" Ra`ah protested, "I have already confessed the truth to you!" Another slap whipped through the space between mother and son as Aziza brought the thin wooden switch down hard across Ra'ah's face.

"You are a liar!" she replied, her voice rising an octave but remaining unwaveringly calm. A burst of several smacks peppered through the air like rapid fire shots as Aziza beat Ra`ah repetitively across the chest, arms, stomach, and legs to the point of her own exhaustion. His denial of her truth was driving her to the precipice of insanity. "You are a wretched boy," she seethed, her voice heavy with contempt for her son's unwillingness to tell a lie.

Ra'ah had shown himself to be a powerful being at a young age, a trait that was of great value to Aziza. However, his sudden departure from under her authority had created an immense amount of anguish and desperation for her, and this was her final attempt to reclaim the control she once held over her child. The words she spoke to him were therefore calculated, inflicting damage that went far beyond the physical abuse of her wooden switch.

Ra`ah attempted to move away from the corner, but there was nowhere to go. Aziza towered over him, her threat moving beyond just the instrument of torture she gripped in her fist. She was his mother. She carried him in her womb and nursed him at her breast. She was his genesis, and an innate sense of honor and reverence for this rooted Ra'ah to where he stood. Indeed, it was this strength to endure that overshadowed the mercilessness of Aziza, and it enflamed and fed her fury.

Ra'ah knew what his mother desired, and his refusal to yield it made her blind with hate. "Mother, what more can I say to you?" Ra`ah beseeched her, holding his arms extended as if welcoming another blow. "I have confessed all!" Another red streak blossoms across the tops of Ra`ah's open palms as his mother violently brought the rod down over them.

Aziza's face was rigid, her eyes cold and hard. "You selfish child! You dishonor me," she countered, "and god. You will be judged for your arrogance and refusal to speak the truth."

Neither of them would openly name the underlying desire of Aziza's words. She saw her son as a wild stallion that must be broken before it could be of any use to her, and his unwillingness to submit his goodness borne out of freedom and joy to the reigns she wished to place on him threatened the power she held over—not just Ra'ah—but the rest of her family. The accusations continued to climb in volume as she stood like a mountain, unmovable in her mission to extinguish the flame of life she saw flickering inside this willful boy. The place she desired to hold in Ra'ah's life was reserved for God, and his refusal to surrender such power to her came at a great cost.

If she could not control him, then she would shatter him, and Aziza was not to be satisfied until his head was bowed, his eyes darkened, and his spirit splintered. There was nothing in that moment that could be said or done to change or redirect her exploitation. She had an agenda, and Ra`ah was to endure her wrath until it had all been thoroughly spent. Ra`ah, unwilling to run and incapable of laying a hand on his mother, withstood her cold and intentional torture, but with each blow that fell, the hard shell required to protect his flame of life, grew thicker and thicker, like a callus that kept out both the ferocity of hate and the tenderness of adoration.

"I would not be a loving mother, Ra`ah," she said, striking him hard across the face with the thicker end of the branch, "if I was passive to your sin."

Aziza and Aaron
(1240)

"Who said you could be here?" he asked, his voice full of accusation and revulsion, a jailer waiting to turn a key in its lock or a laborer preparing to cleanse the land of detritus.

"No one. I simply . . ." Aziza's response was cut off by the smug presumptions of the self-proclaimed doorkeeper to the holy sanctuary.

"Then leave this place! You desecrate it with your presence, woman."

Aaron, an unremarkable, pious-looking man of small stature and an overly scrubbed face blocked Aziza's path with his arms crossed in rejection. His body, face, and eyes all said the same thing: this was not a place for her; she did not belong, and she was unwanted in her present state.

"If," he continued condescendingly, "you will go and purify yourself, then you can come back."

The small man turned to skitter back up the steps of the temple. "Otherwise, you may not pass through this entrance."

Aziza stood silent at the base of the long flight of heavy, white marble stairs, her eyes filling with hot tears that slowly began to spill out despite her best efforts. Shame clamped down like a crocodile around her throat, and she backed away from the entrance to her last beacon of hope. The crowd continued to move around her, like water around a boulder in its path. They moved up effortlessly to this place that she herself was unable to ascend. Side glances of judgment and disdain landed continually like cold, hard raindrops, soaking Aziza in a shower of humiliation. She had been marked as the unwanted and unacceptable, and all present not only knew this, but affirmed it with their looks of contempt.

Aziza stood firm momentarily, keeping her eyes fixed on the back of the man who was intoxicated with the power he held over another human being as his steps seeming to grow lighter as he climbed higher and higher up the sharp incline of stairs. He knew just as well as she did that for her, purification would be impossible. She was, from the inside out, filthy, diminished in value as defined by her way of living. Heaviness settled familiarly onto Aziza's shoulders as she had grown accustomed to it doing, and after taking one last look over the expansive glory of the shimmering temple, Aziza turned and walked away—accepting, finally, that she was indeed, too far gone to ever be readmitted into the presence of God.

Aaron and Levi
(1180)

*A*aron stood alone beneath a single tree, its branches scraggly and sharp, like tiny blades, jutting into the dusty red air of the desert. Off in the distance, a beige cloud of the cracked clay marked the location of the man for whom Aaron believed he was waiting. The thump of his heart strengthened and quickened, causing his chest cavity to throb from the visceral display of a longing he had grown accustomed to feeling but which now seemed reinvigorated at the sight of his approaching solace. The bliss of union that he anticipated caused his whole body to begin to chime, like the mere mention of a lemon causes the cheeks to pucker and the mouth to salivate. Oh, to be seen. Oh, to be held and adored just as he was. This was all Aaron longed for, and it seemed to be making its way to him steadily down the beaten, red road. After several moments of waiting, all Aaron's patience had been spent, and he took off down the hill from his waiting spot beneath the tree to meet the traveling red cloud. Aaron could not help but break into a wide-toothed, uncontrolled grin that unwrapped all his feigned loftiness and vanity. He was simply spilling over with joy.

"Zachariah!" he called, waving both arms overhead like a young albatross endeavoring to lift off the ground for the first time. The cloud began to dissipate as the approaching man slowed his horse's pace, drawing near to Aaron. As the dust settled, the identity of the traveler became clear, and Aaron halted abruptly mid-sprint; the exuberance that had quickened his heartbeat continued its rapid pumping with a new nauseous wave of disbelief. The man sat rigidly atop his horse's back, cloaked in a dark gray hood. He dismounted and swept the covering from his head, revealing a flinty countenance, worn dark by the sun and time.

"Son," the man said shortly, his tone as hardened as his expression. "It is time to come home."

Aaron balked, still reeling from the abrupt pendulum swing of overwhelming emotion. "I have no home, Levi," Aaron snapped, his eyes flashing with anger to keep back the tears that were threatening to push past his lids.

The darkened man did not flinch away from his son's venom or apparent renunciation in the use of his first name but turned his attention toward his horse that stood heaving from the heat and exhaustion of the intense ride in the desert. "That may be," Levi said, stroking the muzzle of the beast, "but you do have a place—a place where you belong. You have a high calling."

A bead of sweat budded on Aaron's forehead. Whether it was from the hard run in the blistering heat or the immense weight that Aaron felt being placed on his shoulders was unclear to him though he suspected it was a combination of the two.

He shook himself and turned away contemptuously. "It is not a calling I can hear. God does not speak to me."

Levi turned from his horse and took several steps toward his son. "Then you must open your ears and your heart to Him!" he said adamantly. "Do not turn your back on this life, Aaron. It will result in your ruin."

"I *am* ruined!" Aaron cried, spinning around to face his father. "Abba, do you not see me?"

Levi stood motionless, looking solemnly upon his firstborn.

"You have never seen me! You are blind to my heart, my longings, my person!"

"I am not blind," Levi said grimly, looking deeply into Aaron's pleading eyes. "You cannot have the life you are pursuing, Aaron."

He had not finished speaking before Aaron screamed, "Then I don't want life! This isn't living! The person I am told I must be is not a living version of *me!*" Aaron beat at his chest as he said this, his tears finally coming forward in uncontrolled waves, "You want a dead version of me, Abba!"

"It is this life you are choosing that leads to death!" Levi said interrupting his son's screams with a raised voice of his own, both their eyes were wide with rage and hurt.

Aaron's shoulders loosened, and the blood from his face that had become inflamed with fury drained away. His fight evaporated, and he turned away to move toward his waiting spot on the hill. "Then no matter what," he said, walking away, "I am dead."

Levi stood silent for a moment before saying quietly, "He isn't coming."

Again, Aaron halted abruptly, his heart suddenly dropping to his stomach rather than drumming out of his chest. Unwilling to believe his father or that he knew the story that Aaron had believed to have been kept hidden, he asked, "*Who* is not coming?"

Levi exhaled heavily then said, "The man whose love you would choose over serving God."

Uncontrolled sobs burst out of Aaron's chest as the sudden realization that his last hope of being fully seen, known, and loved had come crashing down around him in shards.

"You will never see Zachariah again. The choice to wander the desert or to come home to your place at the temple is yours." And with those final words, Levi remounted his steed and rode away, leaving Aaron to stand alone in the dust until it settled.

Levi and Agnes
(1120)

*L*evi pounded continually with his spade into the trunk of a root, giving his all to clear away the obstacles that lay between him and his mission of building a stone wall. The sun was high, but the blessed breeze ministered to Levi repeatedly, brushing his sweat away with its soft strokes of cool air. He had made good progress over the last several days, clearing stones and digging a trench to set the foundation of his wall upon.

Though young, Levi had already proven himself to be capable of accomplishing much. He had vision and resilience that were unique for most adolescents his age and as a result, he had been entrusted with increasingly larger and more important projects. The stone wall that he was laboring to bring forth was to serve as a boundary for the pastured animals of his family's master. Levi was loved by his master, and he knew this. It gave him an immense amount of pride in his work and heightened his desire to please the man for whom he toiled. Though the tasks were often challenging and physically demanding, Levi was continually fueled by the thought of his good master smiling approvingly at the end of his labor, laying his large, gentle hand on his shoulder, and praising him for his love poured out in service. Indeed, Levi was still small in stature and not yet even fifteen; nevertheless, his master respected and honored him as a man, and for this, Levi adored him.

"You've done much work already today, Levi."

Levi jerked his head up in response to the unexpected voice of his master's wife, Agnes. Though she frequently could be seen moving about the estate, walking through the gardens and groves, Levi had never seen her venture into the pasturelands. There was little reason why she should. Disoriented from being caught off guard by her sudden appearance and equally uncertain of what to say, Levi simply nodded and returned to his work. Her presence made him uncomfortable, and he wished her to leave as quickly as she had arrived.

Agnes, however, seemed to be in no hurry to depart. Instead, she stepped closer, holding up a skin of water. "I thought of you this morning when I walked out into the heat. You must be thirsty."

Levi looked back up, suddenly aware of how dry his mouth was. He nodded again and took a step toward Agnes's extended hand to receive the water she offered. Agnes watched Levi as he poured some of the clear, cold water into his mouth, smiling brightly at his acceptance of her offering. When he had finished drinking, Levi offered the skin back to Agnes, but she held up her hand.

"Surely, it is not enough to simply drink the water. It would feel good to pour some of it onto your hot skin."

Levi touched his forehead with the back of his hand, brushing away some of the sweat that had blossomed there. Pouring a small handful of the cool water into his palm, Levi lifted and wiped it over his flushed face.

"Oh, Levi," Agnes said laughing enthusiastically, "you care too much about waste!" Taking the skin from his hands in a playful manor, she said, "let me show you how it is properly done."

And lifting the skin of water over Levi's head, she tipped it upside down so that it poured its entire contents over him. The water soaked Levi, running down over his face, chest, and shoulders. Levi closed his eyes for a moment to keep the water from running into them, and as he did, he felt the warmth of Agnes's body press against his own and the pressure of her soft lips on his. Shocked, Levi withdrew, rubbing his face madly as if to undo what had just occurred.

"What have you done?" Levi asked, utterly bewildered by what was happening. Agnes stood coolly, her eyes slanted in a calculated and seductive way.

"Simply what I've wanted to do for quite some time now," she replied, swinging the empty skin back and forth rhythmically.

Levi continued to rub his face and head, now intensely agitated by the water that had just a moment ago felt like refreshment. "You're betraying your husband," he finally said, still unable to make sense of the situation he now found himself in.

"No," Agnes said, taking a step toward Levi and placing her hand on his chest. "You are. And if you say anything to him about this, I'll be sure that he knows the truth of this moment." Agnes's eyes grew dark briefly as she spoke these words to Levi, and then as if a cloud had passed by, they brightened again.

"I'll bring you more water tomorrow," she said and then turned to walk back up to the beautiful house of Levi's master and her husband, leaving Levi to finish his work in the fields.

Agnes and Julia
(1070)

*J*ulia set her daughter down on the packed earthen floor of their small home. Next to her, she placed a wooden bowl with a hunk of cheese, some dry bread, and a handful of olives, and beside the bowl of food, she placed a bowl of water.

Agnes watched her mother, her eyes wide and uncertain of what was happening. Julia threw some of their tattered blankets onto the floor in a pile then did a slow spin, looking over the dingy, dimly lit room. Agnes continued to search for her mother's eyes, but Julia would not look at her. Instead, Julia patted her daughter's head stiffly, doing her best, it seemed, to prevent any emotion from moving into her body. A small bag full of unknown contents sat by the door of their home.

Agnes continued to watch, still confused by her mother's

strange behavior. After begrudging her daughter this meager show of affection, Julia took up her bag and opened the
door. Agnes leaned onto her palms to push her stout little
legs into the standing position, then quickly toddled over
to her mother, her arms extended, asking to be lifted up.
Julia paused, setting her bag back down; she picked Agnes
up and carried her back to the plot of earth where she had
first placed her.

"You cannot come with me," Julia said firmly.

And standing again, she walked quickly to the door, lifted
her bag, and pushed the door open. Agnes felt an overwhelming panic rise in her chest and immediately, she clambered
back to her feet, but before she could reach her mother, Julia
departed and slammed the door shut behind her. The sudden
realization that she was alone caused Agnes to burst into
tears. She wailed and cried, pounding on the rough wooden
door with her pudgy, tiny fists. She stood there, screaming
and pressing on the door with all her might, trying to either
bring her mother back by calling to her at the top of her
lungs or to reach her by breaking out of her cage. But all her
effort was not enough; the door stood closed, and Julia did
not return.

Agnes cried and screamed for hours that night, until sheer
exhaustion caused her to lie down at the foot of the door,
whimpering softly to herself. She would remain on the floor,
quietly sniffling until she would suddenly be reminded of
how alone she was, and then Agnes would find the strength
to stand back up and continue her efforts of crying out for her

mother to return to her. The night dragged on, and Agnes remained in her cycle of torment, terrified by the horrors that come with abandonment.

Day finally broke, but Julia did not return. Anguish consumed Agnes. There was no comfort for the terror that plagued her for every minute of each day and night that passed. The food and water that her mother had left behind dwindled, and Agnes grew too weak to cry out. After five days of torture, Agnes laid her small head down on the packed earth, giving up hope for rescue. She was soiled, emaciated, dehydrated, and utterly depleted of energy from begging for help at the foot of the wooden door that had been closed on her. So, when there was a knock on the door of her home, Agnes could not respond. A second knock was followed by a call for her mother.

"Julia? Julia, are you home? I have not seen you for several days, and I've grown worried."

Another rap on the door came, and Agnes mustered the tiniest of sounds from deep in her chest. It was enough for the woman standing outside the door to hear, and she pressed in.

"Oh! Agnes!" The woman exhaled in horror, swooping toward the dying toddler like a bird from a great height. "God forgive us," she whispered, wrapping Agnes in her arms hastily. "You are not alone, child. You've been delivered."

Holding Agnes's limp form close to her chest, she departed from the prison, crying with a voice stronger and louder than that of Agnes's, for aid.

Julia and John
(1040)

*J*ulia looped her arm gingerly through her father's arm, stepping into his stride so as not to break the pace of his brisk walk. The evening was slowly exchanging its warm yellows and vibrant oranges for dusky pinks and deep violets as the sound of the birds grew fainter and fainter. Julia and her father John would often take strolls such as this at the end of the day after John had finished another long day laboring in the fields.

John was a small man in stature, with sharp eyes and a gentle spirit, but his temper was not a difficult one to stir. When he would return home at the end of the day, he would first ask his wife, Simone, to join him for a walk in the fields and when she predictably declined, he would turn to his favorite daughter for companionship. Julia, unwilling to stir her father's wrath and equally concerned about protecting him from rejection, would almost always agree. John confessed many things to Julia on these walks—his visions for the future, his disappointments with the present, and his disdain for the past. Julia served as a good listening ear, which was in part why she was his favorite daughter of the seven that he fathered. Her docile spirit was pliable enough to mold into whatever shape he desired at any given moment, be it an attentive friend, gentle counselor, or doting spouse. Julia sensed innately the importance of her role as the caretaker of her family's caretaker, so she never stepped out of her place, though she often paid for it by being alienated from her sisters and receiving venom from her mother who also perceived her daughter's place of honor in the heart of her husband.

On this evening, however, John seemed despondent. His feet dragged heavily across the dirt of the beaten path, as if they were weighed down by some unseen burden. Julia spoke lightly, inviting John into a more joyful disposition.

"Did you notice that the jasmine has finally blossomed outside the window of our home, Abba?" she inquired. "It has the most delicate petals, and when I draw close enough to smell it, the scent makes me want to both fall asleep and dance at the same time."

John only offered a weak smile and patted his daughter's arm lightly. "That's lovely, Julia," he said quietly, looking plaintively across the field.

A little yellow serin hopped through the tall grass, apparently taking in the last of the light that still dappled certain patches of the earth. "Shall we dance now?" Julia asked, turning to face her father, her eyes bright with the life that all little girls possess before it is extinguished.

John turned toward his daughter, and with a deep sigh nodded agreement. Julia wrapped her arms around her father's neck, and they began to spin slowly across the field, with Julia leading. As they danced, Julia sensed the weight begin to fall off her father's shoulders, and a lightness returned to his step. Feeling triumphant, Julia stood on her tiptoes and pulled her father's face down close to her own to give him a kiss on his cheek.

When she drew back, John's eyes were full of tears, and his brow was deeply furrowed. He stood with his lips pressed into a thin line, unwilling to let the emotion burst through. When he finally was able, John looked into Julia's eyes and with a tearful smile said, "You always know what to do. I could never live without you, Julia."

John and Marianna
(980)

ohn and Marianna flew up and down the riverbank, laughing like the water that ran downstream, sliding lively over smooth rocks as it went. The pair took turns picking up oval stones off the shore and exchanging them for the other to skip across the smoother surfaces of the water's face. When one succeeded, the other would rejoice and clap their hands together in celebration before they would return to their search for the next perfect stone. Hours flew by like seconds as the two young children reveled in their play and company.

Marianna was John's older sister by three years, but they could not have been closer in spirit if they had shared the womb. They traipsed up and down this part of the river regularly together, but on this day, John spotted a bird of a type he had not seen before; it was hopping farther upstream than they usually ventured. John was not only naturally curious, but he also possessed a deep love for birds, so it only made sense that he would journey closer to get a better look at the mysterious winged creature.

A broken path of stones led them farther up the river to where the churning of the water was rougher and louder. Marianna, though naturally playful was also a cautious and, at times, timid creature. Sensing danger, she grabbed John by the arm as he continued his advance and, raising her voice so that it could be heard over the now thunderous sounds of the river, she yelled, "Do you think it is a good idea for us to go this far upstream, John? The water is very swift here."

John simply jabbed his finger in the direction of the bird and replied, "Look! We're almost there! Do you see him? He has a white head and black body like he's wearing a cloak!"

John continued to venture farther in, moving offshore and onto the exposed rocks that stood above the water's surface. Marianna, the faithful sister, followed closely behind him, doing her best to ignore the frothing water that, to her, looked ravenous for something to devour. They moved systematically from one stone to the other until finally, John reached the bird that sat perched on the broken limb of a fallen tree in the middle of the river. He bent himself low, looking intently at the color of the bird's feathers, its eyes, and the shape of its beak.

"Marianna!" John called, looking back toward his sister who was still a few stone leaps behind him. "Look!"

Her concentration on landing safely on the rock ahead

of her faltered for a moment, and she slipped and fell hard. Her spine slammed into the point of a neighboring jagged boulder. Marianna cried out in pain and then lay still, her body contorted unnaturally. John clambered down from the rock he stood on in a panic and made his way back across the stones, trying to reach his sister as quickly as he could. When he arrived at her side, her eyes were wide with terror, and tears streamed down her face.

"I can't move at all, John. Get help! Get help, please! I can't move!"

Marianna and Iunia
(930)

*I*unia paced the stone floor of her home, wringing her fingers together anxiously as she whispered in a hushed tone to herself. The corridor was still except for the movement and sounds that echoed from Iunia tittering gently down the hall as she fretted up and down its length. Blazing torches lit the passage in a golden hue, causing the stones to look like they were made of gold. Iunia paused for a moment to place her hand against the cool surface of one of the stones before the clank of the metal gate in the courtyard opening startled her and caused her to turn abruptly. With that, the arrival of the one she had been anticipating was finally announced.

"Iunia! Are you there?" a woman's soft voice floated down the passage reaching Iunia where she stood, still tense in her posture but visibly relieved to hear the voice.

Iunia called out in an equally hushed tone. "Yes," she replied, barely raising her volume above that of a whisper. "I am in the corridor."

The clanking sound of the gate closing rattled through the air, and not long after, it was followed by the appearance of a woman's round, rosy face. Her head was draped in a turquoise shawl, and an expression of genuine concern was etched on her forehead.

"I came as quickly as I could," she said, rushing toward Iunia with her palms open to receive her friend. Iunia embraced her eagerly.

"I do not know what to do," Iunia said, her eyes wide and her breath shallow.

The older woman, though not tall in stature, brought a weightiness with her presence that made Iunia feel over-whelmed and at peace at the same time. "We must ask then," she said confidently, holding Iunia's hands tightly and look-ing deeply into her eyes. "What is the trouble, my friend?"

Iunia shook her head sorrowfully, as fresh tears sprang forth. Rubbing her belly with her eyes downcast, Iunia con-fessed, "I am with child."

The woman stood silent next to Iunia, still holding the hand that had not been pulled away to touch Iunia's stom-ach, which now housed a new life.

"Who has fathered this little one?" the woman asked slowly, her eyes remaining gentle, but fixed.

Iunia choked back a sob that attempted to burst forth before composing herself enough to muster, "I do not know."

Her gentle friend placed both her hands firmly on Iunia's shoulders before pulling her to her chest, holding her firmly as a mother would hold her daughter, and together they wept.

Moments slid by as water passes the riverbank, until Iunia, with great anguish, said, "It was a beautiful moment until it wasn't. Who will ever want me if I have this child? My life is ruined."

Iunia's friend pulled away just enough so that she could reconnect her gaze with Iunia's before saying, "A new life is always a gift."

Iunia shook herself from her friend's embrace angrily and turned away, her eyes now full of tears of anger and her face hot with rage. "I said *my* life is ruined. Perhaps this child would be a gift to the world, but it would be at the cost of my own existence. I don't want to have this baby. I need your help."

Iunia turned again to face her friend, her expression now hard and stony. "Help me get rid of it. I know you can. Please, help me."

Her friend stood, for a moment, her own eyes now full of deep grief and torment. Placing both her palms firmly against her forehead, the woman leaned back, seemingly overcome with a sudden ache in her head.

"Iunia," she says finally, her voice strained but nevertheless strong, "I cannot help you end this life that has begun."

Iunia turned away in hurt and anger, ready to depart before her friend continued, "But I will take this child and raise it as my own if you will only carry it."

With her back still turned, Iunia paused, her hands clenched into fists and eyes shut tightly. Stillness pervaded the space before, "Curse this child!" rang into the air.

Iunia's friend put her hand to her heart before moving toward Iunia. With tenderness she raised Iunia's chin so that she could, once again, look into the young woman's face. "You are not alone, Iunia," she said gently.

Iunia's anger broke for a second time into sorrow, and she said, "If it is a girl, her name will be Marianna." The older woman's eyes filled with question for a moment, but she nodded in agreement.

"For she has brought me much bitterness, but she is also beloved."

Iunia and Andrew
(900)

*I*unia sat at the table across from her mother, sister, and baby brother, watching intently as he gnawed fervently on the bottom end of a wooden spoon. Drool dripped from his tiny chin, and his chubby legs kicked enthusiastically as he flexed and splayed his toes repeatedly. Iunia's mother's eyes were blank as she stared at the unmoving door of their home, a steady backdrop upon which shadows cast by the dancing firelight shone.

Iunia knew that her mother was thinking of Andrew, her husband and their father, wishing he would push his way back into the home and join them for dinner. Nevertheless, each family member knew as well as the other that any hope for his arrival within the next hour was both slim and foolish. His absence had become a frequent occurrence, and Iunia had learned not to ask of his whereabouts. Her questions seemed to distress her mother, causing a wave of both grief and anger to wash over the household like an unexpected tsunami that came crashing from somewhere far out in the distance of her mother's mind.

Iunia's thoughts had shifted from her father to the plate of food in front her when Andrew suddenly pressed into the house as if in response to her withdrawn attention. The whole family was startled. Iunia watched her mother's face wash with sudden emotion, a tenderness that was soaked in ache edged around her lips and filled the center of her eyes before she registered the expression on her husband's face. Iunia despaired as all the blossoming hope in her mother's face iced over like a freezing crust spreading over an arctic lake, clenching the struggling tendrils of love and desire so tightly that it strangled them.

"I am leaving," Andrew said, crossing the short distance from the door to the room that he once shared with Iunia's mother. Her mother did not follow him but turned her attention to her own plate of food, angrily stabbing a piece of meat.

"I thought you had already left," she replied carelessly, giving as little of herself to the man in the other room as she could.

A short, dry laugh floated from the room followed by the sounds of shuffling baskets and the rustling of garments. Andrew reemerged with a full satchel and a flinty expression on his face. Iunia sought his eyes with her own, begging him to look at her, but his gaze was fixed on everything but the faces of his children.

Iunia's father moved back toward the door of their home, and as he passed the table, he dropped a piece of parchment by her mother's arm that cradled their infant boy. She glanced at it and then, in a rage, leapt from the table, her cool and apathetic facade shattering like a fragile mirror.

"You coward!" she screamed, blood pouring into her face so that it turned deep crimson. "You built this family, and now you are turning your back on it!"

Iunia struggled to find a place to land in the middle of the impending battle, seeing no sign of refuge in either of the people with whom she had sought refuge in the past.

"This is a mistake, Andrew! If not for me, for the children. Please, don't abandon us." Iunia's mother's rage dissolved into deep despair, and she crumpled to the floor weeping.

Andrew stood motionless before his wife for a moment, looking at her with a painful amount of contempt. The tension built exponentially as the seconds passed, with each of the children sitting motionless and silent, holding back tears that they dared not release.

Finally, Andrew broke the silence, and leaning his face close to his wife's snarled, "*You* were my mistake. And so was everything that came from my union with you."

Without a glance toward Iunia or a single one of her brothers and sisters, he spun on his heels and departed.

Andrew and Kaira
(860)

The sound and smell of salt wrapped around Andrew like a sheer garment, spinning and dancing gracefully over each inch of his skin. Kaira, his brother's beautiful new wife, stood off in the distance, watching as the waves crashed endlessly on the shore. The bliss of the oceanside seemed to be crushed by the juxtaposing throb Andrew felt in the pit of his stomach as he watched Kaira move slowly away from him, her bare feet leaving a steady trail behind her as she advanced down the coast. Giving in to his desire for her company, Andrew ran to catch up with her, keeping, as he always did, a respectful distance.

"Here, Kaira," he said casually, offering an exquisite pink and white seashell to her. "These are your favorite, are they not?"

Kaira smiled brightly and accepted his offering, brushing his hand lightly with her own as she took the treasure from his palm. Andrew's heart leapt into his throat from nothing more than the sight of her delight. The touch of her skin on his felt like white heat, as if a lightning bolt had just struck him squarely in the chest, and he fought to slow the pounding of his heart.

"They are!" she exclaimed, examining the shell with genuine interest. "You have an eye for beauty, Andrew," Kaira said, looking into his eyes in a way that gutted him.

Indeed, I do, Andrew thought to himself, as he watched her turn the shell over in her hands with admiration. The pang of unquenchable desire erupted painfully within Andrew, despite how hard he fought to squash his feelings.

Andrew had been introduced to Kaira upon the announcement of his brother's engagement to her, and he had learned to love her soon after. She was, to Andrew, the most beautiful human he had ever encountered. The envy and simultaneous devotion he felt toward Kaira's new husband, who was also his brother, had trapped Andrew in a prison from which he knew he would never be able to escape. He had come to accept that he was to remain forever on the outside of a marriage to the woman that his body and heart told him was the love of his life, witnessing the union of what he felt to be his other half with that of another. Andrew leaned into the reality of who he was to Kaira, hoping that the sobering truth that he was never meant to call her more than friend would, in time, erode his longing for her. But this did little to ease the pain of the prolonged and agonizing process of that erosion.

"Kaira!" the voice of Andrew's brother floated across the ocean breeze, pulling his wife back to his side where she belonged. Kaira looked into Andrew's eyes again with her deep blue ones that matched that of the sea by which they both stood. He took note of this and imagined himself drowning in them. Indeed, he felt helpless in their depths, unable to return to the safety of the shore. And Kaira, like the consuming waves, was oblivious and indifferent to his slow, futile death.

"Thank you. I shall treasure it forever!" she said before departing and running toward the call of her husband. Andrew smiled softly to himself, then turned his back to face the ocean so that no one would see the tears that streamed from his eyes.

Kaira and Delilah
(840)

*R*ain spattered the walls and windows of the stone building in which Kaira sat, holding her small knees to her chest and squeezing herself into as tight of a ball as possible. An orange cat lay curled up by her feet, its face twisted toward the ceiling with what looked like a smile of satisfaction etched over its soft, striped face.

She heard Delilah call her name again, but she remained on her perch by the window, unwilling to give way to the hope for a new beginning. The sound of feet pattering softly down the corridor leading up to her room was followed by the click of a metal latch and the sound of the door swinging on its hinges. Delilah stood in the doorway, her worn and darkly tanned face pleading with Kaira to emerge from her hiding place.

"Kaira! They are here!" Kaira shook her dark hair violently and buried her face in her hands.

"I do not want to see them, Delilah," she protested, scooting her small feet closer toward her to form a tighter ball.

"This is foolishness," Delilah said, crossing the room and pulling one of Kaira's hands away from her face. "They have journeyed a great distance to meet you."

Kaira pulled her hand back and despite herself, began to cry. "What if they do not like me? Just like all the others?"

"The others liked you just fine," Delilah interrupted, her demeanor shifting from exasperation to tenderness. "It was simply not the right match." Delilah paused, considering the direction she wished to take in her rebuttal. "Perhaps it was the Lord's will that you find your home with this family, and not the others."

Kaira shifted her eyes up, searching Delilah's for the lie. "I am tired of not being wanted," Kaira whispered. "It hurts so bad."

Delilah knelt in front of Kaira and took both of her hands into her own. "Oh, hush," she chided, pulling Kaira in for an embrace. "You are special, Kaira. We could not give you up to just anyone who wanted a child."

Kaira sat still for a moment, considering this before asking, "But has anyone ever even asked for me? Was there ever a chance for you to deny someone's wish to bring me into their family?"

Delilah paused before letting out a long exhale. "Please,

Kaira. Will you come meet them? Simply put your trust in me."

Kaira sat in the lap of her guardian and friend, fighting the temptation of surrender with everything in her. The risk of betrayal was great, and everything inside her body told her that to listen to Delilah was foolishness.

Nevertheless, after another long moment of sitting together in silence, Kaira nodded her head and stood to her feet. "That is my girl," Delilah whispered, brushing Kaira's hair from her eyes affectionately.

The pair emerged from the room together and entered into the adjacent room where a tall, dark-haired man and a shorter, modest-looking woman stood side by side.

"May I introduce to you, Kaira," Delilah said proudly, placing both hands on Kaira's shoulders as she gave her the slightest encouragement to step forward. Kaira watched as a marked expression of disappointment spread over the faces of the man and woman standing before her.

"It is a girl," the man said, disdainfully.

"What we mean . . . ," the woman interrupted, "is that we were under the impression that you had a little boy that was in need of a home."

Kaira turned her neck so that she could look up at Delilah's face. Her lips were pressed into a hard line, and Kaira saw what looked like a mixture of fury and guilt in her eyes. "It was communicated," Delilah replied through gritted teeth, "that I had a *child* in need of a home under my care."

The man shook his head angrily and turned away. "Such a long journey for nothing." He seethed as he departed.

The woman looked sorrowfully at Kaira for a moment, standing awkwardly in the room, which felt like the air had just been sucked from it. "I do apologize," she eventually mustered.

Kaira could tell that this woman wanted to offer her some sort of consolation, but there was nothing left to be said. Bowing her head, the woman turned and followed after her husband, leaving Kaira and Delilah standing alone in the empty room.

After a long silence, Delilah stepped toward Kaira and placed her hand on her small shoulder and said, "My dear, I am so sorry."

Kaira did not move, and to her own surprise, neither tears nor disappointment arrived. She felt, she imagined, quite a bit like the shells she would collect by the ocean. Empty and unimportant.

"That is alright, Delilah," Kaira said, a strange relief settling over her. She felt the final blow land on her hope, ending her battle with it. It lay dead, never to rise again, and she was now free to move forward.

Delilah and Akiva
(770)

A small group of children stood off in the distance, chasing one another and shrieking with glee. The trees swayed uniformly in a circle, as if acting as audience to the display of delight taking place in the center of their clearing. The sun was still high and beat heavily down onto the browned shoulders of the boys and girls, and there was not a brow that did not glisten with the sweat that resulted from their merriment. Delilah stood next to one of the witnessing trees, herself also taking up the position of observer rather than participant. Her feet felt as if they were full of fluttering wings that wished to lift her up and carry her into the gaiety, but she hung back, uncertain of how she may be received.

Eventually, another young girl who looked to be about the same age as Delilah ran closer to the perimeter upon which she stood, moving into the shadows so she was no longer blinded by the brilliant sun. As the girl's eyes adjusted, she caught sight of Delilah, and with a seeming thrill of delight, squealed. She had found another friend from which to flee! The little girl turned and ran away, and Delilah, knowing as children do, what was wished of her, gave chase as she herself erupted into a fit of giggles and shrieks. Delilah was led into the thick of the mayhem and, with no explanations, was absorbed into the game of cat and mouse.

The minutes moved quickly when set to the tune of joy, and though Delilah had felt herself weary upon her arrival at the field, she found a new lightness that she had not experienced before in her childhood. Her home was not one of light. Indeed, it often felt very dark and heavy, with a spirit of fear and restlessness constantly crouching in the corners of every room. She had often borne witness to the life led by her peers from the outside, hiding where she could, whether on the docks by the sea or within the crevices of the alleyways of her city, and she hungered for the levity and goodness she saw. Now finally, it seemed a hand had been extended toward her in invitation, to join the table and experience the taste of life.

"Atalyah!" a new voice broke into the play, and immediately all other sounds dissipated. The little girl who had first noticed Delilah halted abruptly and turned in the direction of the call.

"Yes, Abba?"

Akiva, a man robed in black with long fringes and an

ornate frock strode into their midst, his nose lifted disdainfully. "It is nearly sundown. Come and wash. Where are the flowers I sent you to fetch for shabbat?"

Atalyah motioned toward a bunch of wild vetchlings, sage, and bellflowers that lay bundled together near Delilah's feet. Akiva's eyes landed on the florals and then traveled to Delilah, focusing in on her face like a predator searching out its prey.

"You!" Akiva snapped, his voice booming with authority. "What are you doing here?"

Delilah felt caught, a surge of shame and guilt that she could not fully comprehend rising out of her stomach. She instinctively took a step back and searched her playmates' faces, looking for an explanation from one of them. What *was* she doing here? But as she sought their eyes for validation of her presence, she found that they either looked away or held the same contempt that she saw painted plainly across Akiva's face. Had they not, just moments ago, been smiling and laughing with her . . . welcoming her with their delight?

Delilah suddenly felt quite foolish, recognizing for the first time that no words had ever been spoken to invite her into their game. "You are not welcome here, gentile," Akiva pronounced as he took a step toward Delilah, shooing her with his hand in a manner that made her feel like a dog begging for scraps at the market. "Away with you."

Delilah did not protest, but turned immediately and fled the field, leaving all the goodness she had gleaned from her time among the children strewn in her wake.

Akiva and Marcus
(720)

*T*he heat could be seen radiating off the dry, parched
earth, the illusion of hazy, shimmering waves causing
everything to look like a vaporous vision that would
disappear with the first sign of wind. But no wind came, and
no rain either. The chapped ground seemed to suck any source
of water or energy from the very beasts that traveled over its
crust. The eyes and faces of each creature, whether man or
animal reflected a desperation for something to breathe life
back into them. A young boy, Akiva, sat on the ledge of the
steps to his home, watching the road that brought travelers
to and from their town.

Akiva liked living on the outskirts of the city, for it gave
him a way to pass the time when the air was too thick for play
and too hot for sleep. He would sit on this perch for hours,
bearing witness to all who entered and all who exited by way

of this road. The minutes seemed to pass by quickly in this place, as if there was something magical about the way time moved between the steps to his home and the world that stretched before his feet just past this threshold.

But on this day at this time, he had not been there long before a traveler came down the road and caught his eye. The shimmering haze, which made every man, woman, and animal look like a figment of the imagination, did not seem to rest on this man. Akiva saw something solid about his presence, something he could not put his finger on, but that made him infinitely curious. Standing to his feet, Akiva shaded his eyes and tried to get a better look at the traveler. As the man drew nearer, Akiva saw that his face, though dirty and tired, did not possess the marked depletion that seemed to weigh down every other pair of eyes he had seen pass by throughout this drought.

Akiva's curiosity won out and before giving thought to his action, he raised his arms over his head and shouted to the old traveler, beckoning him to come over. The traveler looked up at Akiva as he called, an immediate smile spreading over his face, which caused the little boy to glow from the experience of being seen.

"Greetings, friend!" the old man said as he approached Akiva.

The sound of an unfamiliar voice outside her home drew Akiva's mother from inside the house, and she opened the door to step out next to her son just as the traveler arrived at the front of their steps.

"Greetings," she said, looking at the old man in question.

Sensing the confusion that he had just created, Akiva offered his name, smiling brightly at the stranger and then sheepishly at his mother.

"A joy to meet you, Akiva. My name is Marcus," replied the traveler.

"Is there water where you come from?" Akiva asked abruptly, his curiosity about Marcus spilling out irreverently.

A look of playfulness danced over the old man's face while Akiva's mother, whose interest seemed to be equally piqued, half-heartedly shushed him, torn by her desire to appear to be a disciplinary mother as well as to hear the answer to her son's probing question.

"Are you thirsty?" Marcus asked, his eyes suddenly quite sincere.

Akiva nodded fervently, his mouth feeling drier from just the thought of a cool drink of water. "There is not water from where I have come, no," Marcus replied. "But I have tasted of the living water, the supply that will never run dry."

Akiva's mother's eyes narrowed; her curiosity being replaced immediately by skepticism.

Oblivious to her change in demeanor, Akiva pressed farther. "Where can we find this living water? Our land is so dry."

Marcus nodded his head understandingly. "This is why I have come," Marcus replied. "It is my desire to share this living water with you, your family, and anyone else in your city who will receive it."

Perplexed, Akiva looked about. "You do not carry any-thing with you," he observed, daring to hope that he may have his thirst quenched soon but unsure of how.

Marcus shook his head and somewhat sorrowfully replied, "I cannot bring you rain, my son. But the water I offer will not evaporate or leave you for long bouts of time. It will not come and go with the seasons. Indeed, it will carry you through the drought. It is the living water of God, the Spirit of Him who was sent to us as the man called Yeshua."

At these words, Akiva's mother grabbed her son's shoul-ders and ushered him back into the house, shooing Marcus away with her hand before she closed the door behind them.

"Mother, I do not understand. Who is Yeshua? Where can we find His water?"

Akiva's mother stood a moment, her face red with anger and agitation. "He is a deceiver," she replied after a moment, her temperament slowly shifting back into a calm state. "There is no water. He seeks only to divide and tell the same lies that a man who died a long time ago once told."

At this Akiva began cry, his hope for relief from this unbearable drought shattered. "I am so thirsty!" he sobbed, pressing his small hands to his eyes.

His mother, with pity and care, bent down toward him and drew him in for an embrace. "As am I, my darling," she said, "but we must remember what is true and remain faithful to our god. That man is a dangerous gentile. You will encounter many in this life, and you must guard against them and their temptation and the false hope that they offer."

Marcus and Augustine
(650)

*M*arcus woke suddenly with a start, his brow drenched in cold beads of sweat as his chest heaved air in and out rapidly, his lungs pumping in desperation for escape. But escape from what? Marcus took his hand and rubbed it from his forehead down the length of his face. His eyes were wide, scanning the darkness for any remains of what had just been at his heels, somehow threatening his life with nothing more than its presence. Leaning forward, Marcus braced himself over the ledge of his cot, doing his best to slow down the rapid beating of his heart.

Many nights had passed since these dreams had found him, and he had learned to dread the fall of darkness. It felt, he imagined, like whatever it was that terrorized him as he slept, lurked not far off, just behind the border of the trees that surrounded his home. It would wait for him to drop his guard as his eyelids grew heavy, and just as he would fall into slumber, so too would he fall under attack. Marcus rose to his feet and ventured forward, feeling his way in the dark to where he instinctively knew the latch of his bedroom door to be. Grasping the handle, Marcus inhaled deeply, fighting to let the last of his panic fall off him before he emerged from his room. The air seemed lighter as he passed over the threshold of the door, and Marcus felt his shoulders relax and his brow loosen by just a fraction more.

Peace seemed to settle over his frame for a moment before a sudden movement on the stoop outside his home caused everything inside Marcus to leap back to high alert. Had his dreams been a foreshadowing? Had the terror of the forest found its way to his home? Marcus's fists clenched, and his shoulders drew together, instinctively preparing for a fight.

"Marcus?" the voice of Marcus's friend and mentor, Augustine whispered from just outside the door, and Marcus let out another exhale, this time out of exasperation from the overwhelming pendulum swing of his nerves.

"Augustine?" Marcus asked, opening the entrance of his home to his friend. "What are you doing here? It is deep into the night."

Augustine stepped carefully through the doorway, putting great intention toward finding sure footing in the darkness. "I was told to come and see you," Augustine replied, his tone bordering on one of surprise that Marcus had not expected him.

Marcus lit a candle and set it on a table in the center of the room, then motioned for Augustine to sit, doing his best to welcome his friend into his home despite his disorientation. "You were told?" Marcus asked, rubbing his eyes tiredly, still trying to shake himself back into a steady state.

Augustine only nodded his head while straightening his tunic. The pair sat alone in the stillness for a moment before Marcus broke it.

"My friend, I am sorry, but I am still very confused."

Augustine looked at his young friend for a moment, contemplating, it seemed, the best approach to take with his next words. Finally, as if changing his mind about tact, Augustine asked, "Have you had any visions of serpents of late?"

Marcus stared hard at his friend, not at all sure what to make of his sudden appearance and now odd as well as timely question, "Yes," Marcus confessed finally. "Yes, I have had many dreams about serpents." Marcus paused considering for a moment how much he wanted to impart. He added, "Such a dream was what woke me from my sleep just now."

Augustine nodded his head, apparently unsurprised by this news. "Well then, brother," Augustine replied, leaning forward, and placing his hand on Marcus's shoulder, "let us go before the Sovereign, with the help of His Spirit."

Marcus placed his hand over Augustine's hand, which rested on him, and bowing his head, he opened his ears and, to the best of his ability, his heart to the words being spoken over him by his wise and kind friend. Hope, however, for relief and freedom, was something Marcus felt he could

not fully take hold of. Marcus's past was riddled with darkness, and the monster that had recently been at his heels in
his dreams had been pursuing him long before this night.
Indeed, it seemed to Marcus that as soon as he emerged from
the womb, the chase had begun. Marcus was now weary,
ready to finally lie down and be devoured. His fight, he felt,
was coming to a close, for he had no strength left.

His father was a drunk, his mother was gone, and most
of his brothers and sisters had disappeared over the years
into various shadows. An immense beast had devoured those
who came before him in his lineage and now, it seemed, it
was his turn to surrender.

When Augustine had finished his prayer over his friend,
he lifted his wrinkled, watery eyes to meet Marcus's and said,
"Now in peace, lie down and sleep."

Rising to their feet, the two men embraced and went
their separate ways—Augustine back out into the night and
Marcus back to his bed. Lying down, Marcus took another
deep breath, and with great effort, settled himself back into a
state of stillness. It was not too long before sleep befell Marcus once again, and he found himself walking through the
forest of his dream. Fog spun slowly around his ankles and
the bases of the trees, casting a white haze over the ground
and shrouding what lay beneath it. Instinctively and without
much effort, Marcus bent down and seized the floor of the
forest as if it was an immense Persian rug, and then with a
strength he had never felt surge within his being, he lifted
it to reveal an enormous coiled, snake. The snake raised its

giant head, flicking its red tongue threateningly. Marcus detected that the creature was shocked by its exposure, and he watched as it moved into a posture of defense, doing its best to recover from the surprise of being discovered. The serpent reared its upper body preparing to strike. And then Marcus felt it settle over him, like a garment that has been placed over his shoulders, and Authority was bestowed. With a mighty hand, Marcus reached out and through a power he had never known, he ripped the snake from where it lay and crushed it. The creature crumbled as if made of dried clay, and Marcus released its disintegrated remains to the ground before turning and walking away from the forest. As he did, he saw the light of the coming sun begin to march onto the horizon, and he opened his eyes, awakening to a new and beautiful morning.

Augustine and Rachel
(590)

ugustine gasped sharply as another shooting pain stabbed him in his abdomen. The sharp exhale instigated a fit of coughing and in a matter of moments, Augustine was bent low to the ground, his face red and vascular from the strain of heaving air in and out of his exhausted lungs. His fight for air proved to be too much for his weakened stomach, and he began to wretch over his own feet, losing the last of his meal to the ground. Utterly spent, Augustine slumped back against the wall of his home, closing his eyes in an effort to stop the room from spinning. How many months had it been since he had stood on his feet with strength? How long ago was it that he could move without pain, walk without effort, breathe without fighting for his life? His body had betrayed him, and the form that once served him now proved to be a prison of torment. He had had a vision for his life—one of adventure, beauty, and vibrancy. It was a stark contrast to the dimly lit, gray room in which he found himself sitting, isolated in decay.

Lifting his gaze from his soiled feet to the ceiling over his head, Augustine sighed heavily and whispered, "Let it end."

He had been the only child born to his mother and had himself, never married. The years of solitude and quiet had been lonely—not what he would have chosen, but he had learned to manage his deep longings for human connection with time spent among the animals and wild vivaciousness of nature. His routines brought him comfort in knowing what to expect with each new dawn, but the sharp decline in his health had made them altogether unviable. Simple tasks had become overwhelming, and what had once required moderate effort on his part was now entirely impossible. The absence of any care or attentiveness to his basic needs made the lack of relationship and human connection even more apparent. His home was cold, silent, and empty, much like a tomb, he imagined.

"Oh, Lord, am I as alone as I feel?" Augustine whispered, his voice weak and rough, made raw from the constant coughing that had racked his body over the last few months.

He was too young to have lost his strength in this way. His life had barely begun, it seemed, and now he was confined to his home, barely surviving on his own. Another fit of coughs overwhelmed Augustine, and he bent forward onto all fours, fighting for the air of life that he no longer desired to live. When the fit ended, Augustine rested his forehead to the ground and closed his eyes, too weak to right himself. After a moment, he moved his hands slowly toward the perimeter of the room and began to crawl toward the opposite wall, seeking the rest that his cot offered. As he clumsily made his way across the room, he knocked over a stack of parchment, and the leaflets fluttered about the dwelling, like a burst of white doves that had been released from their cage. Ignoring the blunder, Augustine continued forward, seeking only respite from his pain and effort. When he reached his cot, he collapsed onto it, letting out a deep exhale of relief. As he shifted his weight in search of a comfortable position, he heard parchment being crumpled beneath him. Augustine fished his hand down beneath his side and pulled out a small yellow letter that he instantly recognized. It was the last note his mother Rachel had written to him before she passed. It was short and written with a scrawling hand.

"My beloved Augustine," it read, "I shall be journeying on soon. I leave with you all I have to give, which is this blessed reminder that there is no darkness thick enough to hide you from the love that holds you fast. Peace and grace be with you, my son. All else is an illusion."

Augustine scoffed and tossed the letter to the side. His illness was anything but an illusion. His life was being cut short it seemed, and his end was neither slow nor painless. Closing his eyes again, Augustine took as deep a breath as he dared without instigating another fit of coughing.

"An illusion . . . ," he whispered. "My pain and torment, an illusion?" He felt death crouching at his doorstep. It was

the realest presence in the room with him, not the spirit of
the God his mother had served and from whom she claimed
he could not escape. Death was what he could not outrun,
not love. He had sought love his whole life, and it had been
as elusive as the wind.

Opening his eyes, Augustine breathed in deeply again,
and to his surprise, submitted this petition: "If I was meant
to be a vessel of your Spirit's love, then empty me of death."

Rachel and Josiah
(520)

Rachel's mouth was open wide like a roaring lion's. She screamed as loud and hard into the darkness as she could while the rain drenched her face, pelting her like arrows from heaven. There was no room for words in her protest, only the guttural explosion that had been building inside her for the past decade of agony.

Was this it—a life of striving, of wrestling, of being crushed by one wave only to surface for enough air to carry her through as she was devoured by another? Why was she continuing in the fight, she wondered. Her fury had no place to be received, and so she hurled it into the abyss that was nightfall, daring anything to approach and meet her in battle. She did not care if she lost the fight; her only wish was to sink the full weight of her disappointment, grief, and rage into the flesh of any willing opponent. But no such opponent showed its face, and when her screaming was met with nothing but the stillness of the night and the sound of rainfall, Rachel collapsed to her knees and buried her face in her hands, weeping at the agonizing indifference of the world in which she found herself existing.

"I am here!" she finally yelled, looking up into the drops that fell from the blackness to kiss her skin. "Meet me, you coward!"

Was this the kind of God she had chosen to serve? One that flung injustice and trial down from great heights with no explanation or aid, only the cold indifference of rain. "Who am I to you?" she finally whispered, beads of water slipping over her lips as she spoke. "Do you delight in my torment? Or is it worse? Do you not even see me?" Her knees pressed into the mud, her weight digging into the softened earth to create a nest of muck.

"You said that you care for the sparrows," she said, fighting to believe that she could bend the ear of the One she had once trusted would care enough to listen. "Would that you have but made me one; then perhaps I would have learned to rest in that truth."

Leaning forward, Rachel thrust her hands into the rich, black earth and scooped two giant fistfuls of mud up before raising them to the sky. "Prove to me," she screamed, staring into the darkness as streams of water fell across her face and down her neck, "that I'm worth more than this!"

She cried, flinging the mud across the empty, open field. The rain continued to fall, and the time continued to slip by, but Rachel remained in the field, yielding to exhaustion as she fell asleep in the thick, cold earth, the flightless bird, nestled in its crude nest.

The sun was breaking over the ridge of the distant mountains when she finally stirred, her clothes drenched and her face covered in streaks of drying earth. The rain had ceased, and a white haze of fog was rising from the ground all around her. Rachel opened her eyes just enough to let the first rays of sunlight in before she realized that she was not alone. The kind, wrinkled eyes of her aging father Josiah met hers as she awoke to the dawn. His damp hair and muddy garments suggested that he had been with her for hours, sitting by her side as she slept in the rain.

"My daughter," he said, "arise. Let us go and eat."

Rachel looked at her father for a long moment, all her questions rising to her mind instantly. How had he known she was away from home, much less where to find her? How long had he been by her side, and for what reason? But a quiet assurance that she did not understand smoothed the confusion, like a soft hand over the spine of a bristling kitten. Her father had found her and was now asking that she join him for breakfast. It was enough. Picking her soggy self up off the ground with great effort, Rachel stood and stretched her arms again toward the sky, releasing to the best of her ability, the stiffness that had settled over her frame as she had slept in the mud.

Josiah and Hannah
(450)

osiah sat next to his brother, holding his tiny hand with his own. The children were no more than two years apart but Josiah, at the age of six, had already found a calling in his care for others. Large, round tears beaded and dripped off the tip of his baby brother's nose, his small face cast to the floor in shame. Josiah offered no words of comfort, but simply sat patiently by his side, letting the warmth of his body and presence work against the loneliness he sensed to be crouching on the perimeter of their union, waiting for Josiah to retreat so that it might devour the little one who wept. With this awareness, Josiah remained faithful, rigid in his determination to be there for the one he loved and to renounce the lie he innately knew would be whispered in his brother's ear: "You are not wanted."

Many moments passed with the two young boys sitting side by side, holding one another's hands, until their mother Hannah approached them. She paused for a moment and smiled softly, taking in the display of affection as merely a tender expression of childish goodness, never comprehending the profound impact made by Josiah's innocence. Eventually, Hannah bent down toward the younger brother and broke the silence.

"Will you come with me?" she asked, her voice calm and gentle, with no hint of a threat or anger betraying her. The little one nodded his head sheepishly, his eyes still caste to the floor. Hannah extended her hand, and her son pulled his own small one from Josiah's and placed it trustingly into his mother's.

The two walked away from where Josiah sat perched on a rock, but not so far away that he could not hear the words being spoken. Hannah bent down next to the cool, still body of water that stretched before them and pointed her finger to the reflection being returned on its glassy surface.

"What do you see here?" she asked her son, looking at his face as he looked at the water.

"I see water," the little boy said, somewhat confused by his mother's question.

"Yes dear," Hannah replied with a hint of laughter behind her words. "But what do you see *upon* the water? What do you see in the reflection?"

An enormous smile spread over the face of Hannah's four-year-old son as he looked back at his mother joyously,

"I see us! Together." His tiny eyes began to fill with a different kind of tears before his mother cut him off.

"Yes. And now, show me the face of the little boy that I saw you become just a few moments ago."

Josiah watched confusion wash over his brother again as he looked into Hannah's eyes that somehow appeared flinty. "When you were angry," she continued, "and when you were hitting and yelling. Make that face again."

The little one's countenance fell somewhat, but he did his best to obey and with great effort and a noticeable amount of shame, contorted his expression into one of rage.

"That," Hannah said, pointing to the reflection of her son's angry face in the water, "is not my son."

The little one's face fell again, and the crocodile tears returned.

Josiah, who had been sitting on the rock the entire time, hanging on his mother's every word, exhaled with a shudder, mourning for the pain he knew his brother must be feeling and vowing to himself that he would never do anything to be disowned in this way himself.

Hannah and Zephania
(380)

*T*he moon had been in the sky for hours by this time. The night was clear, and the stars were so bright that Hannah thought she may be able to reach into the deep indigo and pluck one of the shimmering jewels right from its canvas should she decide to. Nightfall had become Hannah's favorite time to move and live within the cruel world she had awakened to.

Falling asleep on the packed earth and rising with the sun to the bustle of men and women going about their routines made her lack of a home and family acutely painful. Moving through the city at night, when all was still, quiet, and cool and sleeping during the heat of the day beneath some peddler's cart, was preferable to the alternative of being reminded of her isolation and depravity. Initially, her body had fought the transition to her nocturnal habits, resisting what did not feel natural. Then again, the rest of her existence did not feel at all natural either. It seemed to suit her circumstances, to wake and sleep out of step with what one might consider to be right, for nothing about the life she lived was in line with what could and should have been. This night, however, was set apart from the ordinary. A contradicting cocktail of emotions swirled restlessly inside her gut, creating waves of nausea that would be followed by an enormous surge of euphoric hope.

A small lamp flickered in the window of the tiny dwelling she approached, giving off a warm glow that illuminated only the smallest amount of space. As she drew nearer, the feelings of hope grew fainter, while the waves of nausea seemed to rise in intensity and longevity. Hannah suddenly felt quite certain she was going to be sick and paused for a moment to place her hands on her knees, preparing to lose the meager mouthfuls of food she had scrounged from the waste pile earlier that night.

As she leaned over her feet, preparing for the upheaval, she noticed how filthy her skirts and bare feet were. She was disgraceful—a word that had been placed on her shoulders not all that long ago she realized, though the years she had spent living alone on the streets had felt like nothing less than decades. The memory of her flight from her home was all that was needed to put her sickness over, and she vomited, heaving slowly turning into sobs that racked her bony, fragile frame.

"Oh, please," Hannah whispered into the dark, "receive me."

Meekly and with great shame, Hannah continued forward, growing less confident with each step. When she reached the threshold of her home, Hannah stiffened. Uncertain of what she would say should someone open to her knock. And if the door was not opened, what would she do? Remain outside until daybreak? Her thoughts rushed upon her like a breaking wave, and in a flurry of desperation to cut them off, Hannah balled her hand into a fist and pounded on the rough wooden door. There was only the briefest pause before the door was swept open to reveal her father, Zephaniah.

"Hannah," he said grimly, his face as hard as the packed earth she had learned to sleep upon. "I knew it must be you. Your mother always said you would return at night."

Hannah's eyes filled with tears at the mere sight of her father. She opened her mouth to speak, but her words retreated on her tongue. Instead, the wave of tears rushed forth to choke out all other sounds, and she began to weep, falling to her knees in front of her father. With out looking up, Hannah reached her hand forward and touched Zephaniah's feet.

"Forgive me, Abba," she cried, "I have sinned against you and our family. Please, may I come in? May I see my mother and brothers and sisters?"

Zephaniah stood motionless for a moment. When he finally spoke, his voice cracked with emotion, hints of a deep grief being barred from entrance, seeping into each word.

"Your mother has passed, Hannah. But she always knew you would come back. It was her final wish that we always keep a lamp lit for you. But hear this well; it was you who put her to death. Your betrayal of our family broke her heart so deeply that she was sent to her grave. Do not come here looking for a home. It was by your own hands that it was shattered."

Zephaniah and Portia
(330)

Chickens pecked the ground around Zephaniah, pausing momentarily when their beaks drew near to his feet, considering, he imagined, whether it would be a good idea to take a nip out of them. Zephaniah wiggled his toes enthusiastically, somewhat curious about the sensation of being pecked by a chicken. After extending the opportunity for the chicken's sampling of his extremities a few moments more, Zephaniah picked up his roughly woven basket full of eggs and began to march back up the grassy hill to his family's home. Feeding and watering the chickens and collecting eggs were among Zephaniah's daily chores, and though he had grown tired of the routine over the last several years, he still managed to find joy in the simple and monotonous.

Laughter and joy, he had been told, were two of his gifts.

His seven older brothers were all gifted as well; they had strong opinions and fiery wills that one would not ordinarily cross if anything was known about the brood. Zephaniah's family had a reputation for being of the sort that one did not go against, particularly if you wanted to maintain a good standing within the social circle of their tiny village. The boy's mother, Portia, had been widowed when Zephaniah was no older than three, and she had taken on the role of being head of the home with what, at times, felt like a vengeance. Though Zephaniah's few memories of his father were sweet and tender, the tales he had heard of him were often of the sort that would cause one to think he was neither of those things. But Zephaniah, though he was still quite young, had an inkling that, somehow, both could be true; his father was capable of both goodness as well as evil.

The iron fist that his mother took up after her husband's death had created a dynamic in the family that either drew people in or repelled them, for it was well known that loyalty to the family, and by extension, Portia, was of the upmost importance. Each of the boys had embraced the notion that their mother had had her fair share of exposure to death, and thus they shouldered it as their duty to spare her any extra heartache for the remainder of her days. Zephaniah, being the youngest of the children, had been shepherded into this way of thinking early on, but had never grown entirely accustomed to denying the truth of what he felt and believed when it seemed to conflict with his mother's wishes.

Zephaniah pushed into the entrance of their family home,

whistling a tune as he usually did. Setting the basket full of eggs on the table, Zephaniah scooped a ladle of water from a large jug that sat in the corner of the room and set to the task of cleaning the fresh eggs in a clay bowl. Portia entered the room shortly after Zephaniah had set to task and sat heavily down in a chair across the table from her youngest son.

"Zeph," she said, looking wearily at him, "I need you to stay home with me today."

Zephaniah's enthusiastic scrubbing slowed, and he felt his heart begin to sink in his chest. He knew that when his mother asked this of him, it was usually because the dark clouds, as he imagined them, had settled over her for the day. She was overwhelmed by her own sorrows and needed her son with the most natural sense of levity and joy, to pour himself into her hollow frame, which felt like a cold shell.

"Yes, mother . . . ," Zephaniah replied slowly, "I just . . . ," he paused, peering at Portia sheepishly, uncertain of whether it would be wise to continue. "It's such a beautiful day, and I had wanted so badly to visit the grove."

Portia's face remained blank, her expression giving Zephaniah neither enough confidence to cease or to continue in his petition. Bravely, he continued, "I could bring back a basket of olives! There should be many ripening by now!"

He sat anxiously, a small light of hope for his wish to be granted still dancing in his brown eyes. His mother stared back at him, still unwaveringly void of emotion. "Is that your choice, then?" Portia asked, her words tinged with the smallest hint of venom.

Zephaniah sat for a moment, uncertain of whether this territory he had unknowingly wandered into was as treacherous as it presently seemed. His desires, he felt, were good. How could it be as fraught as all the alarms in his small body seemed to be signaling?

"Yes, Mother, I would very much like to go to the grove today, please."

Portia sat motionless for a moment, not taking her eyes off those of her son before finally, with words as flat and empty as her expression, said, "Very well. Have your way, then."

Zephaniah enthusiastically finished up his chore of washing the eggs before hopping off his stool and grabbing another large basket from the side of the stoop for collecting the promised olives. The grove was many miles from their home, but the journey was part of the reason why he loved his visits there. The sun shone bright and warm, kissing Zephaniah's olive skin so softly that he felt at times he might just curl up and doze. He was as much in love with this land as any man could fall in love with a woman, and he looked forward to his time in it as much as any lovers would long for union. There was a holiness within the olive grove's plot of earth that Zephaniah did not understand but that his feet promised him to be real. He always went barefoot and would often lie down in the tall grass, breathing the air deeply as if taking a long drink of something delicious.

After many hours in the grove, Zephaniah began his journey home, carrying the full and heavy basket of olives along with him. His pace was slower than it had been on his way there since he had to frequently place his burden down and rest. However, he was unwilling to shed any of the olives he had collected, knowing that they were one of his mother's favorite foods. It was nearly dusk when Zephaniah finally arrived home. He began to run toward the stoop of his family's dwelling as it came into view, full of excitement at the thought of sharing the treasure he had carried for several miles with those he loved.

He arrived at the door and set his basket down, taking great care not to spill any of its contents. Zephaniah gave a mighty heave against the large wooden door of their home, but it did not budge. Confused, Zephaniah tried again, but the door was bolted shut from the inside. Zephaniah began to knock on the door, but there was no response.

"Mother! Asa! Amos! It's me, Zeph! Will you let me in, please?" he called.

There was no answer. Zephaniah knocked again and then called out, "I've been locked out! Will someone please let me in?"

A few moments passed before Zephaniah heard a scraping sound and the unbolting of the door. His older brother Asa appeared at the door.

He opened it just a crack and said, "What do you want, Zeph?"

Confused, Zephaniah looked down at his basket of olives and then back up at his older brother, "To . . . to come in. I have olives from the grove."

Asa stared at him and then with a tone as equally cold and void of feeling as his mother's said, "You must remain alone outside tonight, Zeph. I hope this teaches you to never betray your mother again."

And then, without another word, Asa closed the door in Zephaniah's face.

Portia and Asher
(280)

 dark cloud blocked out the sun, casting a shadow over the small group of men and women who stood on the side of the river, each draped in thick robes of black. The three women's faces were covered in veils that clung to their tear-stained cheeks as the wind blew in agitation from one direction to another.

Two men, one older and the other young, stood off just a few paces with the older man's consoling hand resting heavily on the shoulder of the younger man whose head was bowed in sorrow. The three women who stood closest to the river began to kneel, and as they did, the youngest woman who stood in their midst lifted from her chest a small bundle wrapped in linen. The young, lifeless body was placed with great care by the three women into the heart of the grave, dug just large enough for the tiny, precious Ebenezer of the

life lost. Once the infant's head was rested in the dirt, a guttural wail slashed into the air like a sword through a tapestry.

"My son!" the young woman screamed, clutching her fists
to her chest, squeezing them hard as if to protest their emptiness. Her arms should be cradling a baby, not stabilizing
her over the edge of an open grave.

"Portia," the older man by the name of Asher said as he
approached the young woman. "My precious daughter," he
whispered as he knelt next to her at the edge of his grandson's grave.

Wrapping his arm around Portia, Asher pulled her close
so that her face was buried in his chest. Portia wept with
her whole being, at times on the verge of vomiting, and at
others, bringing her protest to such a great volume that the
sounds coming out of her throat felt like jagged rocks as they
rumbled from her chest and out her mouth. All the while,
she knelt with her father, half believing that if she squeezed
her empty arms closely enough to her chest that her child
would somehow return to them.

"His life was precious," Asher said, "and will never be forgotten—not by his mother or the One for whom he was
made and to whom he has returned."

Portia pulled away from her father just enough so she
could look into his eyes, and with gritted teeth asked, "How
can you still bless your God's name? He is a thief."

Asher's eyes, still heavy with sorrow, looked deeply into his
daughter's eyes as tears slipped steadily from them. A silence
hung in the air before reverently and with great tenderness,

Asher scooped up a handful of sand and stones, holding it loosely so that they slipped slowly through his fingers.

"'Cursed is the ground because of you; through painful toil you will eat food from it all the days of your life'."

Asher shifted his gaze from the sand and stones and returned Portia's gaze.

"He is not a thief, daughter. He did not take your son from you. It was the thorns and thistles, the sweat of our brow, the pain in his birth, and the desire you have for more in this life. It is the darkness that pervades this world that we cannot escape. It is not the will of God that a mother bury her child. It is His will that we have life to the full. He was charged as a thief so that your son would not be lost but that someday he may be returned to your arms."

Portia's eyes remained locked on those of her father, but the hardness that protected her heart seemed to break like a crack on a frozen lake, and she began to wail again, burying her face once more into the chest of her good father. Asher lifted his palm and placed it heavily on the head of his weeping daughter and closing his eyes whispered, "Death is not the final word."

Asher and Peter
(220)

There was a lightness in Asher's feet that he had never felt before. His eyes had clarity for what felt like the first time ever in his life. He had been blind though he did not know it, and now, somehow, as if an unseen darkness had been lifted, his vision was restored. It all fell into place like a lock and key that fit together perfectly to unlatch a bolted door.

He ran down the street feeling explosive joy bursting in his chest several times a minute like internal, ongoing thunderclaps. He had to share what he had been given. It was the only thing to do, it seemed. He raced down the darkened streets, passing the old familiar landmarks that somehow felt new and different. Everything was different—the plants, the animals, the buildings, people's faces—everything. Asher had awakened to find himself in an entirely different world.

He ran until he passed the last building on the outskirts of town.

Off in the distance, he could see the fields, all of them ripening so fully that they looked as if they would soon burst if not harvested. The air was sticky and warm, but a crisp undercurrent whispered that cooler winds were coming, and that the time to reap was now. Asher flew through the fields, taking care not to upset too many of the crops he was surrounded by. They seemed to almost propel him onward as he moved, encouraging his mission.

"Go forth!" they said. "Go forth and go quickly!" Asher emerged from the towering fronds of the first field and then, off in the distance, he spotted him, his father Peter.

"Abba!" Asher called. "Abba, I bring you good news!" Peter stood in the field with his arms full of a portion of his day's work. A crooked wooden cart hitched to the family's gentle donkey, Martha, was parked next to him, holding the rest of what his father had already harvested. Peter lifted his eyes to meet those of his son as he approached with gladness. Peter's face was tired and stained with sweat and dirt, but he returned his son's smile with one of his own, reflecting that he was happy to see him.

Asher collapsed to his knees as soon as he arrived before his father, completely breathless but unwilling to take the time to regain his composure before he launched into the delivery of his message.

"Abba!" he gasped. "It is true! All of it!"

Peter set his bundle down on the rickety cart and placed

his large strong hand on his son's shoulder. "Breathe, my son. What is true?"

Asher's eyes glowed brightly as if somehow reflecting a light he had seen. "The stories they tell of the Christ that Rome crucified! He was a Jew, but He did not come just for Jews! He came for everyone! Everyone and anyone who will accept Him!"

Peter stood up, withdrawing his hand. "Do not be a fool, Asher. Perhaps you should pay better attention to the words you yourself just spoke. The man they called the Christ was *crucified*. You know as well as anyone that what Rome intends to kill is killed. They are the masters of death."

Asher shook his head wildly, his dark locks swirling back and forth. "No, Abba! He overcame death! *He* is the master of death!"

Peter turned his back to his son and picked up his sickle.

Asher persisted. "His name is Yeshua! They say He was laid away, thought to be dead, but after three days in a wealthy man's tomb, the entrance was opened, and His body could not be found! Several of His followers saw Him in flesh! It is said He ate food and walked on roads with travelers."

Peter kept his back turned and began to hack violently at the stalks. "Do you not hear the insanity in the words you are saying? Of course, His followers would make claims of seeing Him after He was said to be dead. They had too much to lose with His death. It's a hoax, Asher, and you are fool for listening to the words of liars. These rumors have been circulating for many years now. It is time for them to die."

"They will never die, Abba," Asher rebutted, "for they are true! I believe it with everything in me. I have given my life to sharing the message that the man called Yeshua gave to His first followers. I too want to be a disciple of the One who came back to life after death."

Peter put down his sickle and turned to his son, tears welling up in his eyes. "Then I fear son, that if you will not let these rumors die, it shall be you who perishes."

Peter and Rebecca
(150)

The roar of the crowd was deafening. Men and women in front, behind, and on either side of Peter yelled with raised fists, stamping their feet, and screaming until their faces turned red and their veins bulged. The intensity frightened Peter, but he did his best not to show it. He stood sheepishly beside his mother Rebecca clutching the hem of her garments while staring up into the faces of those surrounding them. Though the looks of rage and what Peter thought looked like hunger were intense and terrifying in some cases, they paled in contrast to what Peter had heard was about to happen.

This was his first visit to the Coliseum, but tales of the harrowing events that took place here had reached him prior to his arrival at this monumental structure. The volume of the screams somehow rose as two enormous iron gates down at the center of the ring began to open. Peter shifted his eyes hesitantly, his curiosity piqued by the mighty gladiators he had heard an equal number of stories about. His breath caught when, instead of an impressive armor-clad force, a motley looking band of men, women, and children emerged from the gaping black hole that sat behind the iron threshold. They emerged into the light, looking wide-eyed and frail, their postures timid and yet somehow welcoming. Peter was about to ask his mother where the gladiators were when he spotted a boy who looked to be about his age clinging to the dress of a woman who must have been his mother in the same way that Peter now clung to his.

A loud voice rang out over the heads of the people gathered, bellowing in revilement, "We give to you, these wretched souls. Behold, followers of King Yeshua!"

The crowd erupted again in thunderous applause and shouts, ravenous for a spectacle.

"On this day, we demonstrate for you the fate of those who find refuge in the dead! The emperor is pleased to give you this triumphant display of his power manifested in the crushing of those who would refuse to give him his honor due!"

Screams swelled in pitch, and Peter saw men, women, and even some children in the crowd begin to fling old food and rocks toward those who stood in the center of the coliseum.

"But behold, your emperor is a merciful one!" the voice boomed again. "Who is your king?" the voice asked. "Take a knee for Caesar, and you shall be spared!"

Peter's gaze was glued to the face of the little boy, plead-ing with him in his heart to come to his knees. He watched as the little boy lifted his eyes to his mother. She returned his look with a smile and a gentle touch of his cheek. She whispered something to him that Peter could not hear, but he wondered at her love for her son. Did she not know what was about to happen? How could she not do what it took to save, not just her own life, but that of her child? The small group of men, women, and children remained huddled together but unmoving. Not one of them said a word or fell to the ground. They stood like rooted trees, looking as meek and powerful as anything Peter had ever seen.

"Shall we show mercy to those who defy Rome?" the voice asked.

The crowd in unison, as if anticipating this question shouted, "No mercy!"

Peter jumped as he heard, from his own mother's lips, a blood-curdling scream, calling for the death of the little boy, no older than Peter, standing just below them in the dust. "No mercy! No mercy!" Rebecca shrieked; her eyes wild with a hate he had not seen before.

"Followers of King Yeshua!" the voice exclaimed, "I give you, your fate!"

And as these final words were imparted, a second pair of iron gates simultaneously opened, releasing a pride of skeletal lions. They walked slowly into the ring, their ears flattened to their heads and their teeth bared to show their yellow fangs. The lions moved methodically, circling the small group of people, still huddled together, holding one another's hands, or clutching their children. The hackles rose on the backs of the giant, starved cats, and Peter watched as several of them leaned back on their haunches preparing to attack. He saw the little boy bury his face in his mother's skirt, unable to look into the deadly eyes of the ravenous animals.

At that moment, Peter also buried his own face into the skirt of his mother who was still screaming for the blood of the group of people at the center of the ring. Just as he did, a blood- chilling snarl ripped into the air from the throat of famished hunters, and the crowd went ballistic, screaming profanity and encouragement to the cats as they ripped into each man, woman, and child.

The crowd jeered and laughed, calling to those being torn apart, "Where is your dead king?!"

Peter felt heat radiating off Rebecca, her body shaking with what he couldn't fathom being anything other than hatred as she cursed and mocked those being devoured before her. Peter began to shake, his body giving into heaving sobs despite his efforts to stifle them.

Rebecca and Rufus
(100)

R ebecca stood idly on the side of the street, holding her sopping sack of wet clothes. She had just returned from the river, and her arms were tired from hauling her wrung-out garments over the miles that led her back into the city. Exhaling heavily, Rebecca used the back of her hand to wipe a stream of sweat from the side of her brow, looking listlessly up the street in search of an opening in the crowd.

This part of town was a difficult place for Rebecca to enter. There were no exterior forces that would keep her from it, but she found herself feeling immensely heavy and full of despair when she stood upon this ground in particular. She had heard tales of this corner of the city. A man once had passed through these crowds on his way to do something amazing, and as he had picked his way along this very street, she had been told that he had stopped for a woman. A woman like herself. Rebecca touched her cheek, suddenly aware of a tear that had escaped from behind her eyes as she remembered the story. Shaking herself, Rebecca reshouldered her laundry and pressed forward, doing her part to keep from touching any who passed, for she was unclean just as the woman in the story had been unclean.

"It is nothing more than gossip," Rebecca told herself, battling the cocktail of envy, desire, and yearning that bubbled up inside her every time she ventured across this road. She avoided it for the sake of her crushed hope, and yet she repeatedly found herself standing in this section of the city, fantasizing against her will, that a spirit or ghost of the miracle worker would find her and heal her as he had healed the other unclean woman.

This man was long gone though, crucified by the Romans, so she had been told. In her distractedness, Rebecca bumped accidently into the side of a feeble, white-bearded man, dropping her sack of clothing in a damp mess upon his feet.

"Woman!" the man exclaimed, hobbling backward, doing his best to distance himself from Rebecca and her spilled, wet garments.

"Forgive me," she said, keeping her eyes down as she hurried to pick up her sack and its contents. "I . . . I was not paying attention."

The old man, Rufus, after recovering from being thrown off-kilter, straightened himself, doing his part to recover his composure.

"A woman like you owes it to her community to keep her distance! I must go and purify myself, thanks to your oblivion."

His words dripped with contempt and disgust—his perception of Rebecca clearly one of disdain. Rebecca did not respond to his rebuke but did her best to recover her clothing, desiring only to move away from this man. The stark contrast between this encounter and the interaction that presumably took place many years ago in the same setting was overwhelming. Her silence, for whatever reason, inflamed Rufus, and he pressed farther into her wounds with his words.

"How dare you pull me back down into your depths of death and decay! Selfish, ignorant woman!"

And closing the gap, he had initially created between himself and Rebecca, Rufus advanced, pulling his arm back to release a forceful slap across Rebecca's face with his right hand.

Rufus and the Rabbi
(20)

ufus stood quietly by a stone pillar, waiting patiently for the reading of the Scriptures to begin. A new rabbi had been teaching at the synagogue, and Rufus was eager to listen to Him.

Many had spoken of this man and his ability to discern the Torah. The eyes of some lit up when they spoke of Him, shining as if they held a new, undying light behind their lids, while others cursed Him with curled lips that drew back in a snarl that made them look almost animalistic. Rufus was not so easily persuaded in one direction or another. Or so he told himself. He was indifferent to individuals such as this man. Indeed, Rufus clung to the notion that he cared very little about this rabbi and the rumors that circled around Him. In truth, however, there was a deep pull toward the new teacher that was inexplicably powerful. He possessed something that

Rufus hungered for though he did not know what it was. He had waited for the Sabbath with great anticipation, knowing instinctively that this day brought something new on its wings. Now, he stood quietly, waiting in the shadows of the back of the room as he had grown accustomed to doing.

Though he was not perceived as contagious or a plague, Rufus was not ignorant of the fact that those who knew him believed his handicap to be one borne out of sin. There was a darkness that reached back into his history somewhere that had delivered him unto this fate. Those who did not know him, changed their disposition toward him as soon as their eyes landed on this shameful part of his body. To keep himself away from such judgment and scorn, he did his best to fade into the backdrop, never seen nor heard, but merely a part of the scenery on the stage of life that unfolded before him daily.

His desire to become invisible vanished instantly, however, when the rabbi entered the room. Rufus felt his pulse quicken and his breath grow deep. When the rabbi opened His mouth, Rufus clung to each word, sensing that there was something more to be gleaned from Him than just the meaning of the words He spoke. Rufus found himself not just desiring to be brought forth from the background but to be seen and known by this captivating human. No sooner had Rufus acknowledged this longing in his heart, than the eyes of the rabbi landed on him, and in a voice of profound power spoken with kindness, commanded him: "Come here."

Rufus's feet obeyed immediately, and he suddenly found

himself standing in the center of the synagogue, looking into the eyes of the rabbi. The rabbi returned his gaze with one of compassion that did not evoke shame in him but, like the warmth of spring beckoning the first blooms to push through the dirt, called forth his hope. The rabbi looked around the room filled with ordinary men and women as well as members of the Pharisees and Sadducees, and then asked, "Is it lawful on the Sabbath to do good or to do harm, to save life or to kill?"

Rufus held his breath, sensing that his own fate somehow was held within the response that was to come from those in attendance. But no response came. Indeed, the room was as silent as a tomb.

Rufus was suddenly acutely aware of how exposed he was, his shame now in the exact place he had sought to avoid all his life—at the center of everyone's scrutiny. Why had this rabbi demanded he come forward? Was he to become an example of what is to be expected from a life of sin? Was he to represent the face of shame? When the rabbi's eyes returned to meet his own, they were full of rage and anger, a stark juxtaposition to what Rufus had just beheld when their eyes first locked.

"Stretch out your hand," He said, and again, without Rufus even realizing what was happening, his right hand obeyed, emerging from where he kept it tucked away in his robe's long sleeve, extending itself toward the rabbi like a snake slithering out of hiding. He was flayed open, the thing that kept him in the shadows of every room and on the sidelines of every human interaction was now laid bare in the light of the synagogue, with every eye looking upon it. His hand was gnarled and rigid, purple, and gray in tone, plainly void of life and possessing no value or meaning. It hung there limply, incapable of carrying out the purpose for which it was first designed. Rufus felt his eyes fill with tears, wishing only to draw his hand back into his sleeve and retreat into the shadows, but when he looked again, for the third time, into the eyes of the rabbi, he saw the same compassion he had first beheld—all His rage and wrath, not gone, but somehow feeding and brightening the ferocity with which He loved Rufus. Slowly, like warm water spreading over the skin, Rufus began to feel life return to his curled, stony fingers, and he realized that in the moment that he had heeded the words of the rabbi and stretched out his hand, it had been restored.

Rufus searched for words of praise, joy, triumph, or gratitude, but his voice was gone. He stood for many moments it seemed, unable to take his eyes off the rabbi, until slowly, without saying anything, he began to back away, anxious to show his restored self to his family and friends. He did not return to the shadows though but ran from the synagogue straight into the sunlight of day.

The Accused

Before reading the following chapter,
consider listening to the song,
"Dark,"
by Fr. Tansi

splintering snap, like the crashing fall of a tree, pulls me out of these moments like a fish on the end of a hooked line. I collapse to my knees, breathless in a new sense—utterly depraved.

"Oh, God," I gasp, once I find it within me.

I look about, my hand now clutching my own exposed chest, where the Brilliant Being's had once been. I wonder at time and whether it still exists. Placing my hands over my head, I begin to rock, utterly confused and full of despair. Had I not asked Him to have His way? And where was He? In the story? In this moment?

I look around, but I feel alone. I now know, at least to some extent, the depth of my own depravity. But where was the healing that I had been promised? I am still the victim and the convicted; my own blood is still pouring from my chest while that of another's stains my hands. I rise to my feet shakily, my being's expansion now experiencing, for the first time, how heavy it could be when met with the full reality of its own shortcomings. I begin to wander in the light, searching for a distraction or source of relief from my exposure. It is not long before I come upon a place where I have been before.

This place is familiar to me, for it holds the same peace and stillness that my favorite corner of the earth held. If ever I felt alone, discouraged, angry, or full of grief too heavy to bear, I would venture into the mountains. They would usher me in with their tall maples, oaks, pines, and poplars, consoling me with their whispering branches and the comforting aroma of earth and life as I climbed into their folds. The mountains would draw me in like a mother's arms, pulling her crying child up onto her lap so that she could hold them in their sorrow. And it was here within the light, as if it had been realized for the sole purpose of my wandering into it, that I would find this same type of haven.

As I venture farther forward, I see that two fallen logs lay parallel to the edge of a reservoir of water. The earth around them is scattered with orange pine needles, while above, the overhanging tree branches pull in toward the center of the reservoir and then up toward the sky as if they are trying to escape from under the towering evergreens that overshadow them. I take a seat on the log closer to me, then sigh into a slump. I had sought moments such as these in the past on earth—moments of stillness and peace. I hadn't known what I was searching for at the time. Perhaps I was merely searching for answers—just a release from the cobwebs that seemed to hang on my frame and brain that made me feel perpetually tired and taut. In any case, I never felt that I came away from my retreats of silence in places such as this with any satisfaction. In fact, I felt hungrier for some form of reassurance or relief than ever.

For some time, I sit staring at the rings in the water formed from dropping pine needles; I am caught between the desire to return to and at the same time forget all the moments of the past that I had just realized to be a part of me. I allow stillness and silence to overtake the space. It is not long after this that the Brilliant Being, quietly, like a wild animal emerging from the forest, approaches. He smiles at me and gestures toward the second log, inquiring if it would be alright for Him to sit. I nod, a little baffled that He would ask. We sit in stillness for a time—neither one of us saying anything, just staring quietly at the body of water before us.

I continue to steal side-glances of Him until I finally turn to Him and ask, "Who are you?"

He smiles kindly and returns my question with another, "Who do you say that I am?"

I feel like I've been catapulted back into Sunday school on earth, with this being the culmination of all my church training. Why not revert to the historically correct response? I shift my weight uneasily and mumble, "Jesus?"

He continues to smile, His eyes now shining with what looks like playfulness. "Yeshua was what my mother called me, but many know me as Jesus."

I clear my throat uncomfortably, before mumbling, "Figured."

I fumble around in my mind for something to say. In the past, when I would pray, I would always say something like, "Dear Lord, thank You for who You are. Please continue to show me Yourself, so that I can become more like You."

But that seemed too formal somehow, and even worse, ingenuine. I know He has been with me, witnessing all that had just unfolded. Indeed, He had seen it all before. And yet here He sits, giving me the time and space to digest it in His presence. How would one of those thoughtless conversational pieces that I would pick out of my go-to basket of Jesus phrases work in this moment? They don't fit, and so my saying something simply would make it apparent that I was just looking for words to fill the space. We remain together in the quiet—me fidgeting, Him watching.

Finally, before I have time to properly mull these words over, I say, "I'm glad You're here."

Yeshua looks at me and smiles. "Thank you," he replies. "I'm glad to be here."

He continues to watch me, still smiling, but there is a quizzical look in His eyes. Quiet took its turn again, until I mumbled, "I don't know what to say."

As if expecting my remark, Yeshua asks, "What do you want to say?"

I surprised myself by having an answer to His question. "That I don't understand. I don't understand any of this. I feel like everything is entirely hopeless, meaningless, and . . ." my voice breaks off as I felt a lump of suppressed emotions bubble into my throat like a pocket of air rising to the surface of water. "Is there a purpose or weight to anything at all?" I ask through tears.

Yeshua's smile fades, and his eyes grow deep with sorrow and understanding. He does not answer my question but rises to His feet.

"Don't go!" I say, again surprising myself with the panic in my voice. He shakes His head and steps toward the log I sit upon. He gestures again, asking if He may share my seat.

Bewildered still at His questioning, I nod, gazing up at His extraordinarily beautiful, sorrowful face. "Beloved," He says, sitting down, "it is not outside the nature of man to be without understanding."

I can no longer look up at Him, but I feel His arm wrap softly around my shoulder. "I am able to hold all your doubts, questions, and fears. You may not understand for quite some time." He pauses and takes my hand, pressing it firmly between His before whispering fervently, "But this does not mean that it shall never be so. I will stay with you until you can see clearly."

I sob and feel His arm around my shoulder pull me into His chest. "You are My treasure. All shall be well."

As we sit, my face still covered with my hands and His arms still holding me closely, my sorrow becomes inflamed, churning with a newfound confidence in my security. These emotions continue to percolate until they begin to spit fury. Hot, angry tears fill my eyes. His promises seem cruel and out of reach. I've not just seen and witnessed the horrors of what my life was built upon, I am now a part of it, and in so many ways, the product of it. I'm disgusted with the gruesome evidence of all the betrayal, selfishness, and distortion of what should have been good that is scrawled over my being like a bad stain.

"You can't make this right," I whisper into the stillness. And I realize, as the words leave my lips, how in so many ways, I fear the thought of His word being kept. For should He reach into this past and erase all that was wrong, all that hurts and wounds and breaks, then how would any of what came from it be valid? My pain and sorrow as well as that of all those who came before me, was a tragedy. To be bound up in a blink of an eye, as if it had not ever existed, would reveal it to be as trivial as sweeping up a broken plate with a broom. Is my grief and sorrow so trite a thing that, with a snap of a Mighty God's fingers, it be undone? I weep, overwhelmed by the impossibility of what I desire in my heart— the reversal of the pain from my dark history as well as its validation.

How can I wish it all gone and still ask that it be seen and honored? I feel my Lord's touch on my shoulder strengthen as I sit in despair, my hands still covering my face.

"Is it too great a task for me?" He asks, His question not presuming He knows what my answer may be.

"Yes!" I jump to my feet, an unexpected explosion of fury and rage erupting out of my chest. My stomach feels nauseous over the mangled parade of darkness I had just witnessed—the wicked prospering, the innocent suffering, and injustice triumphing in my own story.

"It's insanity! You made this whole world! You made every person who has suffered and died as well as every person who has killed and destroyed! You can't tell me that You are justified *or* able to make sense out of any of this waste when *none* of us asked to be a part of this big story that *You* conjured up!"

My fists are balled and my teeth clenched, and a part of me wishes that Yeshua would rise to His feet so that I would feel better about delivering a punch to His face. And as if in response to my unspoken desire, Yeshua stands and offers me His hand again, His eyes full of what I can only summarize as hope.

"I see your wounds, and I knew from whence they came before you were born, Beloved. When I touched them, I gave you the ability to see and experience the depth of sin and evil with which your past is fraught. How," He asks, "Could you embrace all the healing and life I have to give if you do not fully comprehend how deeply you've been wounded? How can you embrace the joy of soaring if you never see the great height from which you've fallen?"

My desire to strike His beautiful face dissipates and is replaced by a wash of utter despair.

"My Lord," I sob, finally relaxing my fists and shoulders,

"I see and understand how much, not just I, but my past, needs to be healed. But . . ." my voice trembles out of both reverence and fear of whom I ask my question. "How can You honor the pain? Is it just a blemish to be scrubbed from memory? A nonevent to be wiped from one's mind like writing in the sand?"

I shake my head in disbelief at my own temerity as well as at the resurrection that I've been promised. I know in whose presence I stand, but I cannot quell my need to have this suffering seen, not just reversed. His hand remains extended toward me, and His eyes, though stormy and dangerous still, remain full of hope.

"Come," He says, "and see.

Consider listening to the song,
"How It Sets You Free,"
by Gable Price and Friends
as a conclusion to this chapter.

Ushered

Before reading the following chapter,
consider listening to the song,
"Light in Me,"
by Laura Lucas, Rod Coote

I reach out with fear and trembling fingers and take His hand. I startle immediately, for as my palm brushes the top of His, a tremendous bellow from above our heads begins to shake the place upon which we stand.

If we had been on earth and I were still alive, I would have described the experience as an earthquake, but this shaking did not come from beneath us, but above. It rumbled and growled like the sound of an enormous beast that has been awakened from its sleep until it erupted in a climactic chorus of trumpeting. The sound cleared the air of all the noise that had been whirling within it, though I had not noticed any sounds before, along with all the tumult in my own head, which up to that point, had been budding off worries, doubts, and fear.

The trumpeting is joined by the sound of voices singing words that I had not heard before though I understand the meaning behind their rejoicing.

"Behold your God!" they proclaim, chiming like clashing swords and whistling as wind over mountain peaks.

My Lord begins to ascend and I, with my hand still in His, ascend with Him. I see His full transfiguration begin to take place, a tremendous, glorious, frightening sight. I feel the air knocked out of me and indeed, there is no longer any breath in my lungs. I am, in essence, a shell, hollowed out of my frame and soul before the Creator. I gasp and struggle to reclaim that last breath, fearing that the longer I go without being able to inhale, the more likely it is that I might vanish altogether into a vapor. But breath eludes me, being beckoned away toward the gravitational heave of the Glorious being I call my God. Everything within and around us is being sucked, like a tide toward the depths of the sea, into the undeniable Glory from whom all things were made and by whom all things are being beckoned to return.

Within this transfiguration, I see the etchings of all that has ever been and is and is to come swirling like a mighty ball of energy and held together by the One from whom their existence was first spoken. I feel myself growing brittle, like a dried leaf or frayed strand of hair, and I fear my proximity to my God, by whom I once felt upheld and nourished—the vine from which I grew—would prove to be my end. I try to cry out but find myself unable to do so without any breath in my lungs. In that moment, with perfect clarity, I realize how desperately and absolutely I desire nothing more than unity with my designer and sustainer. And though I never knew it before, I realize that this is all I ever have desired. I feel myself caving in on my own hollow frame, now crumbling, breathless and disconnected from its life source. Claps of thunder and the rushing of wind emerge, not from, but in response to the magnitude of what is happening before my eyes.

I see my Lord, for barely a moment, in what I can't imagine being anything but His full glory; nevertheless, the wiser parts of my being assure me that what I'm seeing is not even a fraction of His fullness. The experience is entirely too much weight for my frame and as I begin to splinter, I hear the voice of my King call me by name.

"Will you, my Beloved, take Me to be your Savior?"

As His words reach me, I feel the immediate sensation of a wash of something thick and wet covering my hands, and I am reminded of the blood that is soaking them.

Another voice calls out to me, asking me, "What have you done? Listen! Your brother's blood cries out to me from the ground."

How am I to respond? My very voice and breath do not belong to me. Indeed, I am a void that is also somehow fracturing in Yeshua's presence, about to fall apart. I look again to the Christ, realizing I have been exposed.

I am naked and fully seen without a place to run or hide.
What have I done? I am reminded of the wound ripped
open in my own chest, throbbing with an ache of profound
depravity and pain. Shall I point to my own mutilation? Is
the injustice that I have suffered enough to save me from
what I am guilty of? I see laid before me the choice that I
must make. Shall I direct all attention toward myself, aim-
ing the culmination of this cleansing swell straight toward
my own, exposed heart? Or shall I reach my blood-soaked
hands toward Yeshua, bringing judgment not toward my
own pain but toward what I myself have done and to the
one in whom I now trust?

I have no breath in my lungs with which to respond,
but I stretch my bloody hands toward Yeshua and instinctively plunge them into His side, drenching them in the
scarlet that pours forth from His wounds. Then, as if
a weight of enormous size had been dropped, there is a
tremendous thud followed by a shudder beneath our feet
that reverberated up my spine. And just as my own breath
had been drawn out of me, my history begins to unravel
like a snagged tapestry. I watch as each moment of my
past story—down to the smallest detail including those
I had forgotten—is subsumed into the glory and terror
of Yeshua. They soar into a maelstrom of chaos, throwing vibrations in directions I didn't know existed. Then,
like flashes of lightning, from His hands, feet, side, and
head, deep wounds open like doorways. They stream
forth light, and each, as it is opened, beckons my story

to enter through it—the threshold to the sacred place of
Christ's dwelling. My story is being ushered into the Holy
of Holies.

Then I see them, one by one—the minutes, hours,
days, and years of my past parade before me and enter
into the sacredness of Christ's own body, just like I had
always imagined the animals entering Noah's ark. But as
I watched the mangled, broken stories limp by, I notice
something that I had not seen before in the stories of my
history's harm. There, within each second is the undeniable presence of Yeshua. His essence, though varying
in shape, tone, and form at each point in time, is overwhelming—so overwhelming that I can't understand how
I could have missed it before. It was wrapped around the
shoulders of Ra'ah, cradling the flame He first lit to sus-
tain its warmth through the coldness of his mother's abuse.
It drew, like an ocean's tide, the reverence and respect of
Henry and his mother to the abandoned infant child. It
seethed at the desecration and molestation of a young girl's
innocence and autonomy while it simultaneously mourned
the emptiness inside the soul of a man who had become
so ravenous for connection that he would breech such an
egregious line. Yeshua was there through each instant, His
eyes not only seeing, but His Being simultaneously taking
on the experience of every wretched soul over whom He
presided.

"I see now," I whisper, for as soon I gave myself over to
the hand by which I had been formed, my breath returned

to me. "You were there," I whisper again, my newly opened eyes filling with crystal tears. "You were there . . ."

So immense was my relief that I thought for a moment I might lift off and float away, as a result of my great unburdening. But I remain, tethered now, in a security that I had not known—tethered to the Lover of my soul and the Redeemer of my life. I watch as the last seconds of my existence soar through the air and enter into the brilliance of Yeshua's magnificence. And as they do, the openings in Christ's body from which the light had come, close like a door, sealing my story with a final stream of the purest crimson.

Yeshua puts His hand to His chest and bowing His head reverently proclaims, "For you, my Beloved, it has been finished."

These words invoke yet another alteration in my being, and my eyes begin to grow dim. My form becomes aware of how utterly depleted it is in every sense, and I realize in that moment that I am being cradled in the arms of Yeshua just as the little girl had been. Indeed, just as her wounds had grown in size and multiplied on the body of Christ, so had my own, which are now, though large and fully open, pouring out that same light into which the young girl had vanished. Upon this realization, the components of my soul, spirit, mind, and form begin to close up shop just as the doors were sealed shut in the hands, feet, side, and head of Yeshua. I sink, like a coffin lowered into the ground, like a ship enveloped by a wave, or an immense stone rolled over the mouth of a cave, into darkness.

Consider listening to the song,
"I Think I Love You"
by Mudhouse as a conclusion to this chapter.

New

Before reading the following chapter,
consider listening to the song,
"Kiss You,"
by Jess Ray

t was the sound you would hear if your head was submerged beneath the surface of the ocean as a wave came crashing over you. It roared mightily, drawing me out of what felt like a deep, deep sleep. Everything was heavy, and I could not move. I lay there, wakening to the sound of this rushing force but unable to stir for the briefest moment of consciousness.

And then I heard Him. He shouted for me. One time, He spoke my name—the one I was never known by on earth but that every cell in my being stood at attention for immediately. He knew me by my true name, and He bellowed it into the depths where I lay weighted down. I was made free to rise instantaneously, and I obeyed His call, walking toward the voice that had just beckoned me. I was guided only by the direction from which I heard my name reborn, and so I walked in it until at last, I emerged from the dark. Time ceased to be as I was held in the suspension of what remains when all else falls away.

*   *   *

I once again adjust my eyes to the light, and I begin to survey the place in which I find myself—a place of unspeakable beauty and glory. It holds hints of a memory deep within the boughs of the trees and tresses of the grass, but no more than what was enough to offer me the warm hug of familiarity. Outside of this embrace that came from recognizing these forms of trees, ridges of mountain peaks, and shores of oceans deep, I could never explain what kind of land I now stood in, for it was undeniably a world upon which I had not before landed. I lift my eyes unto the hills and from somewhere in the mountain range, the sound of something akin to a small child whistling a lullaby floats in increasing volume to reach me where I had once lain supine.

Slowly and triumphantly, the song begins to grow in volume and tempo. It began as a soft invitation and slowly evolved into a call to, not just awake, but to awake and draw near. I want to lift my feet and run as fast and hard as I can in the direction from which the sound is coming, but something told me to wait. It was then, the moment that I tuned into that small inclination of hesitation, that I realized I was not alone in this attunement. I felt the soil beneath my feet churn with life and anticipation. The trees were bending their trunks and boughs in the same direction in which I wanted to throw myself; they were groaning and trembling as if they were about to burst into a thousand pieces. The birds were circling in spirals up and down the ether, or dancing impatiently on the limbs of the eager trees. The stones themselves were somehow emanating this desire that could not be explained with the finite vocabulary of the human tongue, but which I can only describe as a yearning to take off in a dead sprint toward the mountains. Despite burning with expectation, we all remain planted and vibrating with the anticipation of something tremendous, our inner workings whispering the same thing. *Wait for the Lord.*

And it is not long before I become quite glad in my heart that I had chosen to wait, for as I stood on the top of that hill, my eyes scanning the horizon for the source of the song, I saw a warm glow begin to kiss the ridges of the mountains and slowly spread its warmth throughout the entire valley. As the rosy light spread its nourishment, the sound of the small child whistling grew louder and more terrifyingly beautiful, with the glow churning and frothing into an overwhelming wave. The swell was too desirous and powerful to stand before, and I come to my knees, feeling the culmination of the full resurrection of my life. The wave crashed into us like a tsunami, smashing every surface it met like pottery on a stone floor, bringing the land to its knees just as a ferocious kiss on the lips of a ravished lover would. In the same moment that the wave collided, it wove and bound up, braiding every component of what already was with something new. The shimmering tie of light wove itself not just into my own form but also into every rejoicing tree, creature, blade of grass, rock, and piece of fruit that hung from the branches of the trees. A simultaneous exhale of satisfaction and exquisite relief was sighed as, in unison, we found the climax of our glorious reunion with the One from whom we should never have been separated. I recall the bubble baths I enjoyed as an infant. Indeed, I felt like an infant again in that moment—innocent, free, and precious. We were not just awake, but whole, unknotted, and realigned. All the creation around me and I are simply divine. This is it—the ram caught in the brambles, the star shining over a city, the rainbow arcing in the sky. I unclench and release to the arrival. His promise to me fulfilled and my restoration, at last, complete.

As this cleansing wave of new life settled over me and all I was surrounded by, Yeshua was with me. Indeed, His presence was the vanguard of that rosy light that arrested the hilltop upon which I stood.

"It is all new?" I asked Him, my eyes finally looking into His in a way I never thought I would have the joy of experiencing.

He smiled at me and whispered, "It is all as it should be," before gesturing toward our surroundings. "Do you recognize anyone?"

I stare at Him, confused by His simple question. But then I notice . . . just behind his raised arm, about twenty feet from where we stood, the outline of a familiar tree. I blinked and, in a moment, I recognize the apple tree upon which I climbed as a child. Its limbs had held me through the warm afternoons of my younger years, from springtime to fall. And by it stood its sister tree, which due to its closed growth pattern, had not been climbed and swung upon as frequently.

I felt tears begin to well, the response one would expect from seeing a dear friend for the first time in a very long time. And indeed, it had been long. We moved from the home that stood by these trees when I was eight and, in many ways, when I left those trees behind, I left my childhood behind. For it was in and around that house that the sweetest and best memories of my childhood were made. This realization brought my attention to a small field at the base of the hill where overgrown, golden blades of grass swayed uniformly in a wave pattern. A fallen log and patch of wild raspberry brambles on its perimeter confirmed that this was indeed the same one that I had hidden within so many times, as an adolescent, watching the clouds, reading a book, or studying a beetle. And I felt certain in that moment that if I were to enter the field and lie down in its yellow sea, I would find that very beetle, still climbing its towering frond.

I look to Yeshua, not understanding. "Are all the pieces of the forest around my childhood home here?"

Yeshua's eyes brightened like that of a friend who is about to watch you unwrap a gift. "Every piece of my world that has been a part of your life is with us now. Every bird whose tune reached your ears is here. Every stone and plot of earth that you tread upon is here. Every tree that you climbed in or were nourished, warmed, and protected by is growing within this valley. There is not a summit you've reached or simply marveled at that cannot be found within this mountain range, and each animal you befriended, observed, or even passed by unseen and uninterested in, is with us now."

I look about me, bewildered at what my Lord had just said.

"You have another chance," He whispered.

Slowly, we walked together through the gardens, valley, and seaside. I would routinely stop in my tracks and exclaim at the discovery of some familiar creature or place, and I would feel the eyes of Yeshua, my Creator, Savior, and friend on me, watching with delight, like a father would watch his child who is reveling in play. I ask Him questions about how things work, why He made them just so, and what He had in mind when He brought them into existence. All His answers surprised me, and none of them disappointed. We walked until we arrived at the base of one of the mountains at which point we start to climb. This, in and of itself, was an extraordinary experience. It had been many years since I had been able to move without pain and great effort, and even when I was young with strong lungs and confident legs, it took energy from me. Now I found, as I put one foot in front of another on my climb up this mountain, it gave energy. Like a battery being juiced up or a tank being filled, I found the same strengthening nourishment enter me through my climb. It was as if I was enjoying a hearty, healthy meal, only I didn't end up desiring a nap after ingestion.

As we advanced up the rocky surface, I began to hear many voices talking, singing, and laughing as the sound traveled down from somewhere higher up the mountainside. Not long after, an exquisite scent of something I could only imagine possessing the most satisfying flavor wafts from the same direction. The sound and smell possessed all the earmarks of an immense party. I had anticipated a breathtaking view and the familiar experience of accomplishment that would usually follow my hikes while alive on earth, but the realization that we were headed for a celebration of a seemingly incalculable caliber brought on a new kind of excitation for reaching the top of this mountain. As I quicken my pace, I thought I heard Yeshua chuckle.

"Hurry!" I said, for after smelling the essence of the ongoing feast that I suspected was being held at the top of this rock face, I became acutely aware of how painfully ravenous I was.

Consider listening to the song,
"Dawn,"
by Fr. Tansi as a conclusion to this chapter.

The Table

Before reading the following chapter,
consider listening to the song,
"Kinda Wild,"
by JUDAH., Ellie Holcomb

The end of the banqueting hall could not be seen from where I stood. Cedar pillars, golden lamps holding flaming torches, and exquisite fountains lined the walls. Enormous openings filled with painted glass stretched from the glistening marble floors to the boundless sky. The windows poured light into the room like giant buckets of water being dumped out, as a sea of men and women, all covered from head to toe in glory, delighted within the immense room. The doors to the banquet looked so heavy that I doubted any force could move them. They were flung open like giant mahogany arms, inviting an embrace as warm breezes rushed in through them. The zephyr, as if acting as an ethereal waiter, lifted the intoxicating aromas of the decadent feast up into its folds, and carried them back out into the open air, exchanging the fresh scent of the mountains and seaside for the mouthwatering fragrance of the Lord's feast.

A throng of men and women were dancing madly up and down the aisles as circles of musicians sat hammering on their instruments, creating an ethereal symphony proportionate to the abundance that stretched before me. Sweat poured from brows, and tears streamed from eyes as men and women rolled with laughter and stamped with passion. The scene was entirely ridiculous, shimmering with an unforeseen display of exuberant delight. The scent of the feast and the celebration at hand brought me to a carefree euphoria that I had not before known, even during my most physically and emotionally inebriated states on earth.

I turned to Yeshua, hoping to join the dance, but he was already tearing into the throng, laughing hysterically. I ran after Him, taken aback but also not at all surprised, by the natural levity that emerged so suddenly from the same Christ who had, just moments ago, almost disintegrated me by simply revealing a fraction of His Glory. We pressed into the throng, with Yeshua Himself taking my hand and joining it with the palms of those around us, introducing me to those whom I had not yet met and reconnecting me with those whom I had. Someone poured me a cup of a deep crimson drink and in moments, I was entirely immersed in a celebration of never before known triumph. I moved toward the depths of the throng, dancing, and clapping, looking like the child I had always needed to be.

I took another deep swig of the, quite literally, heavenly drink but instantly spat it out in shock when my eyes landed on a young woman and man, sitting side by side at the long wooden table, pouring one another drinks, and talking enthusiastically. I squinted my eyes; certain I was seeing things wrong.

"Yeshua!" I yelled above the din of laughter and tramping feet. I looked for His face and spotted Him participating in something that resembled the London Bridge game I would play as a child. He smiled and lifted His brows questioningly, as if to say, "Yes? What is it?"

I wave my hand dramatically in the direction of the man and woman sitting at the table, entirely flummoxed at what I thought was unfolding. "Is that Eric and Martha?" I yelled, too curious to worry about potentially being heard by the pair of, seemingly, good friends. After all, Eric had been the old sailor who forced himself onto the little girl, Martha, on the ship that she and her family had taken to America. But they both were here, and they were willingly, not just sitting side by side, but engaging in what appeared to be a sincerely deep and mutually enjoyable conversation.

Yeshua's eyes were filled again with that look of blended playfulness and satisfaction. "What do you think?" He asked, clearly enjoying my shock. I looked back at them, trying to make sense of the history of these two people and this moment that they were sharing.

Then I heard Yeshua, standing by my side (the sudden realizations of His presence becoming more and more a normal and expected thing) and, as if He knew the somersaults that my brain was attempting to do, He said, "It will never make sense, Beloved. Because it simply doesn't."

I looked up at Him, His kindness positively radiant and His eyes full of compassion for my slow comprehension. "But this is why I chose to submit my will to the Father's."

I stared for a moment, trying to catch up with His words and feeling, once again, surprised by my own surprise, because although it didn't make any sense, it made perfect sense in light of who I stood next to.

"Is this it?" I asked finally, my eyes traveling from Martha and Eric to the sea of mankind that expanded beyond my sight. I began to find them, sprinkled throughout the throng of colorful, glorious, marked faces—the men and women who had not just been in my story, but had touched it through their existence and presence on the earth. They wove and intersected in the most intricate ways, and like a common red thread, I saw it all connected back to this one God made flesh who stood by my side. It was this Man alone who wove it all together and thus, through Him, gave it all its footing in a history that would never crumble or decay. It was the story of His Glory, handed down to each of us as an inheritance that would never lose its value or be diminished in weight. The pain, the goodness, the brokenness, and the bliss, mattered entirely and solely because of Him. It was the explicit demonstration and articulation of the story of love finally brought to fruition.

"Is it finally over? The waiting, the longing, the . . . story?" I asked.

Again, Yeshua's eyes told me something before His words did, as a light of joy and flame of ferocity flashed over His countenance. "Look, Beloved," He said, gesturing toward the expansive feast that lay before us. "Truly, I tell you, the story will not be over until every seat at my Father's table is filled."

Yeshua lowered His arm and then, gazing off to a place I sensed I had not yet seen, He said, "Not one of my brothers or sisters shall go hungry. Not one."

Closing Song,
"Lion/Lamb,"
by Joshua Levanthal

Acknowledgments

A special song for my beloveds:
"Just Because,"
by JUDAH.

To my older sister, Madeline, whose life is so full of meaning, purpose and beauty; you walked with me through every page of this book, though you may not have known it. The weight of your story is incomprehensible, just like your worth. Open your wings, Butterfly.

To Niki Swann, whose insight, compassion, and servant heart I so admire; thank you for taking time to discuss roadblocks, complex emotions, and the speculative with me over the phone, breakfast, and your own dinner table.

To Zak Foreman, whose artistry, eye for beauty, and sacrificial spirit made my vision for the cover of this book come to life; you are one of my favorite people. I don't think it is a mistake that you played a critical role in the completion of this particular story. The impact of your participation in this world is immense.

To Rachel Bacon, whose willingness to show up on my behalf and serve in the midst of her own difficulties energized and directed my efforts to make the final push toward the finish line. Thank you for your insights, your time, your kindness, and your gift of self. I am blessed to have you in my corner.

To Sam and Bethany Chastain, whose generosity of home, Spirit, story, and friendship served as wind in my sails. Your contribution to this novel could never be overstated.

To Victoria Allen, whose demonstration of strength, resiliency, and wisdom fueled the dwindling fires of inspiration and confidence; thank you for giving of yourself, your story, and your love. Your friendship is one of my greatest treasures.

To Gray Allen, whose stand against darkness fostered a new kingdom of joy, play, and life; your ripple effect is beautiful and powerful. Stay wild.

To my children, Judah, Gwendolyn, and Willow, whose vivacity and brilliance keep me young; thank you for sharing your goodness with me and for serving as a daily reminder of the glory that is to be resurrected.

To my husband and my love, Hunter, whose encouragement, faith, strength, and sacrifice made this entire book possible. Thank you for beholding me and calling the woman I was made to be back into existence. She would never have awakened if not for the voice of the Spirit speaking through you.